PANDORA

ROMANCING A GOD SERIES

CHARLEY MARSH

TIMBERDOODLE PRESS

INTRODUCTION

The Story Of Pandora

In Greek mythology Pandora was the first mortal woman, modeled from clay by the gods. Apparently early man lived a harsh life, imposed on them by those same gods. Prometheus felt sorry for the early men and gave them the gift of fire to ease their lives, angering Zeus. Stingy bastard.

Zeus commanded the creation of woman, beginning with Pandora who he then gifted to Promotheus's foolish younger brother as a bride. Zeus gave Pandora a storage jar for a wedding gift which she of course opened. Who wouldn't? It was a *wedding gift,* for crying out loud.

The rest is well known history. The evil spirits trapped inside the storage jar were freed and have wreaked havoc on mankind ever since.

Our story next picks up in modern times in a small city in the midwest ...

CHAPTER 1

P ANDORA J ONES HURRIED down the dirt alley, a worry clutched to her chest in one slender gloved hand. Her long, midnight blue wool cape—the one fashion indulgence she allowed herself—fluttered behind her and turned her shadow grotesque.

She scanned the bank parking lot that edged the east side of the alley and kept close to the brick store backs that fronted the opposite side, skirting around the awkward metal dumpsters that every business in America seemed to possess.

How many back dirt alleys had she wandered in her short life?

Too many. So many that she was beginning to believe that her entire life had been lived in the dark spaces of La Crosse. And she saw no end in sight. No way out.

The pungent, metallic smell of a quick rain shower on the parking lot's pavement overlaid the fresh sweet scent of the newly opened crabapple blossoms that decorated the open bank lot.

At three in the morning Pandora knew that anyone she met in the alley would mean trouble. Even the cops. How could she explain to the police that she ventured forth every night to collect the worries that plagued the small city of La Crosse, Wisconsin?

They would assume she was crazy and drop her at the nearest Psych Ward, never to be released because there was no family left to release her to.

And maybe they'd be right, Pandora mused, as she reached Albion Street and turned right, away from the river. All of the women in her family, as far back as the earliest recorded human history, had devoted their entire lives to collecting the world's worries and stuffing them back inside the special boxes that they built to hold them.

She blamed her crazy life on her ancestor—the original Pandora who opened the famous box and loosed its contents upon the world.

The original container hadn't actually been a box, but a covered jar called a pithos. Some translator had misread the word in the original manuscript and his translation stuck.

Pandora knew the translator had been a man because a) back then women weren't allowed to perform such important tasks like translating ancient scrolls, and b) no women would have made that mistake. A woman would have been very aware of the difference between a box and a jar.

So the first Pandora had unwittingly released worries and illness and death and evil onto an unsuspecting, and until that moment, carefree world.

Of course, it wasn't really her ancestor's fault. She'd been set up by the almighty Zeus. The jar was a gift, and what woman would not open a gift? Especially a gift from a god. A drop-dead handsome god that enjoyed playing games. The bastard.

Despite the blossoming spring trees, the night still carried a sharp bite of winter's chill on the air. Pandora pulled her cloak tighter around her and held it with her free hand. She wished she'd remembered a hat. Her ears felt cold and her nose ran.

She pushed her arm free of the cape and wiped her nose on her shirt sleeve. Disgusting, but what could she do? Tomorrow night she would remember to carry a hankie and wear a hat.

A car passed by one block over on Winter Street. Bass music boomed from its speakers, pulsing shock waves through the air. She caught the flash of blue strobe lights between the houses and the music abruptly cut off.

She had been wise to take Albion Street home even though she lived on Winter. The cops always patrolled Winter because of the large mansions that filled several city blocks. Early in La Crosse history, Winter Street had been the home of the wealthy, the movers and shakers who helped build La Crosse into the bustling city that it was today.

One of those Winter Street mansions belonged to the Jones family. Her family. Built two hundred and fifty years earlier by Warren Jones, an early La Crosse lumber tycoon, the large stone mansion—more of a small castle really—had remained in the Jones family until passing to the current Pandora, the last of the Jones family line.

The last Pandora. Unless she married and produced more little girls—an unlikely scenario given her current occupation. Where did a nice young woman who slept days and scoured the city every night find the opportunity to meet young men suitable for marrying—or even just mating?

Short answer—*only* answer—she doesn't. The creatures that roamed at night were not good father material.

The very thought that she would be the one to break the family tradition made her want to scream with frustration.

Pandora had been searching for a suitable mate for ten years now, ever since she had turned twenty. Her mother had given her strict instructions before her death. What to look for in a man, what to avoid, how to test a potential candidate.

She had never reached the testing phase. None of her potential suitors ever called back for a second date.

She didn't understand why not. She had registered with a dating/matchmaker service and done everything a woman was supposed to do to attract the opposite sex.

She bathed and perfumed, painted her face and lips, wore the latest fashions, pretended to be interested in whatever the man said, laughed at flat jokes. The list went on and on.

The bottom line was that dating was work. Hard work. She had grown tired of it and then simply stopped because none of the men she dated were very interesting, and who wanted to waste their life on a dull mate?

Not her. Not even for babies.

No, she amended. She lied. At this point she would put up with a lot to create a child. To have family again. There just were no candidates.

Pandora swore under her breath and cut between two large homes that had been broken into smaller apartments. These broken-up older homes catered to seasonal college students, of which La Crosse had many. There were five such buildings on this block alone.

Too many students, in her opinion. The large number of female transients cut her potential pool of mates into a very small number. A number so small that it currently contained not a single specimen.

She pushed down the familiar lump of loneliness and frustration and concentrated instead on getting home unseen.

A soft light glowed in the window of the ground floor apartment on her left. Pandora stopped as she often did, and stood in the deep shadows of the adjacent building while she observed the students who lived in the lighted ground floor apartment.

She knew there was an ordinance against Peeping Toms, and

if she was honest with herself she was breaking that ordinance. Peeping Pandora. How much lower could she sink?

Disgusted with herself, she turned to continue on, but her feet faltered and stopped.

Two men and two women occupied the apartment's living room. One of the women had lived in the apartment for the last two years.

It pained Pandora to know that *this* woman had no problem getting dates. Ever.

She knew this because she cut between these same buildings nearly every night. Their back yards, long since turned into off-street parking spaces, backed onto the grounds of her mansion and provided a way to come and go without being seen.

And nearly every night she saw the occupant of this ground floor apartment entertain a seemingly endless stream of men.

Take tonight. There she was; Miss College Student, a curvaceous blond, wrapping her arms around a thin, brown haired man. They were slow-dancing to music Pandora could barely hear, hips grinding against one another, lips locked as if glued together.

Practically the same scene greeted her every night. Petite, yet curvaceous, blonde with different guy. Every night, a new guy.

What did she have that Pandora didn't?

An intense longing and a deep sense of envy washed over her. Thirty years old and she had never even been kissed. How the devil was she supposed to find a mate and reproduce before she grew too old if she couldn't even get kissed?

While it was true that her people lived longer lives than the average human, they still had the human's limited years of reproductive capability. Her mother had been very clear on that subject while she lived.

"You should have your baby before you turn fifty, Dora. Things get a little iffy after that. Even better, reproduce in your thirties. That's the ideal time. That's your prime for making babies."

Well, dammit. She was thirty. She was ready to go. There were only ten years left of that ideal window her mother had mentioned. With no prospective mates in her past or on the horizon, things were looking pretty bleak for the plight of mankind.

The worries filling the secret pockets in her cape stirred. The ache of longing deepened. The worries drew from her pain and grew stronger.

"Cut it out, Pandora," she said aloud. "You know worries feed on each other. Finish up. Go home." She tore her attention away from the dancing couple and forced her feet to move, slipping through the hedge to her own back yard.

The irony of Pandora's situation never occurred to her. She devoted her life to collecting the world's worries, but who would deal with hers?

CHAPTER 2

"Tough break, boy-o, but somebody has to do it. I'm just glad it isn't my responsibility. One of the perks of being the youngest son, you understand." Pauli punched his older brother in the arm and grinned.

Zee scowled and refrained from returning Pauli's punch. He knew that if he did, the fight would escalate until the ground trembled beneath their feet.

The last time that had happened they had been punished with banishment to the Australian Outback. It hadn't been a pleasant time for Zee, a man who loved his motorcycles, fine food and drink, and beautiful women. Lots of beautiful women.

Of which there were plenty here on the La Jolla public beach where he and Pauli were skim boarding. There must be something in the southern California air, Zee mused, something that made beautiful people.

He'd have to ask his mother. She'd know. She kept track of all that kind of stuff.

The beach was small compared to the more popular west coast beaches, but had the added attraction that it tended to be used by the class of people who shopped the high-end boutiques on the cliffs above.

The type of people who bought small bars of solid gold from street vendors, and didn't blink twice at dropping several thousand dollars for a tiny handbag.

The Beautiful People. People who never asked how much anything cost. People who needed to be seen in all the right places. People like Zee and Pauli. Shallow people.

Zee frowned. Where had *that* thought come from? What was wrong with him lately? La Jolla was crawling with just the sort of people he usually sought out. He should be grooving on it.

He shook off the mood, scooped up his thin, round board and out of habit winked at the pair of beauties walking by him. They giggled and smiled, then stopped. Their second time by in the last few minutes, he noted.

It rarely took longer than that for women to find an excuse to hit on the brothers. They were built in the image of their father, the greatest of the Greek gods. There wasn't another male specimen on the beach who could hold a candle to them.

Both brothers were tall and muscular with their father's classic features: broad forehead, full, sensuous lips, straight nose and strong jaw, intelligent, smoky gray eyes with thick dark lashes.

Only their hair differed. Where Zee's silky, straight black hair, neatly tied back in a short queue, gave him the look of a dangerous man, Pauli's dark curls tumbled about his face in an angelic halo that fit his easy-going nature.

"I get the blond this time," Pauli whispered, skimming up beside Zee and hopping off his board. "Last time you stuck me with the redhead I thought she was going to chew my manly unit off."

Zee grinned at his brother. "Hey, if I remember right, you begged me to let you have the redhead. I told you they could be tough to handle. But no worries, if you aren't man enough, I'll take this one."

The glare from Pauli's eyes only made Zee's grin grow. While the brothers loved each other dearly and would defend one another to the death, they also enjoyed a healthy competition when it came to the fairer sex.

"Hello ladies," Zee said smoothly, "what are two such lovelies doing unescorted on such a prime day? Perhaps my brother and I should remedy that situation, wouldn't you agree, Pauli?"

The busty redhead giggled, her augmented breasts practically jiggling out of the tiny scraps of cloth that barely met the decency laws.

"Polly? Isn't that a girl's name?" she asked in a whispery lisp.

Zee gave an inward sigh. While it was true that he enjoyed beautiful women, he preferred them to have brains. That particular combo seemed to be in short supply in his life lately. He gave a smile that didn't quite reach his eyes.

"Yeah, it sounds girly, but my brother is a pussy, so the name fits. How would you ladies like to join us for dinner and dancing this evening?"

He held out a strong, well-formed hand. "My name is Zee and this handsome loser is my brother Pauli."

The redhead gave him a limp, weak handshake and giggled again when he brought her hand to his lips and brushed them lightly across its freckled back.

"We'd love to have dinner with you," answered the blonde. A typical Californian, she sported the requisite long straight hair, even features, even tan, athletic body. A woman interchangeable with a million other young California women.

Zee realized he had grown bored with the state. It was time to move on. Perhaps his father's directive had come at a good time. At least it gave him a purpose and something to do.

Besides, he'd get to ride his new bike halfway across the country. Thinking of the new motor bike, he smiled and dropped the redhead's hand.

"Great. Why don't we meet you cliffside around eight o'clock? We'll grab something to eat and then hit a couple of the clubs."

They parted ways, the girls whispering and giggling and looking back over their shoulders as they walked away. The brothers returned to their skim boarding.

"That redhead had a great body, Zee. I almost wish I hadn't called the blonde. And did you hear her talk? All soft and feminine-like."

Zee shook his head at his brother, his mouth twisted in disgust. "You have a lot to learn about women, boy-o," he said, throwing Pauli's earlier term back at him. "That redhead was about as fake as they come. Fake body, fake voice. I'm already bored with her and the evening hasn't even started."

Pauli tucked his board under his arm and eyed his brother speculatively. "What's wrong with you, Zee? You're usually full of energy. You love picking up women. You seem sort of . . . flat today."

"I feel flat. I guess I'm just ready to leave this place. Father's errand came at a good time, I think. I'll head out tomorrow. How about you?"

Pauli's eyes gleamed. "Oh, I'm sticking for a while longer. I'll take the blonde out tonight, but I'll set up a date with the redhead for later in the week since you don't want her."

He punched Zee lightly on a well-formed bicep. "You can always call me if you need any help with the mysterious errand."

"Yeah, like that will ever happen."

The brothers smiled at each other good-naturedly. They were very different, and at the same time very close. Best friends as well as brothers.

Feeling better, Zee tossed his skimboard onto the receding surf and leaped on it.

CHAPTER 3

PANDORA SLIPPED through the gap in the wooden fence that separated the rental properties from her own yard. Standing against the fence, she carefully searched the mansion's treed grounds for movement.

Seeing nothing to alarm her, she ran to the rear entrance and let herself into the mudroom.

Under normal circumstances, the massive Jones mansion, four stories of pale yellow limestone fashioned into round turrets and large, square, sunny rooms, would be far too large for one small woman to occupy.

But Pandora Jones's circumstances were far from normal.

She removed her cape, scooped the worries from its interior pockets, plopped them into a waiting box, slapped down the cover before the other worries could escape, and kicked of her worn leather boots.

Energy efficient night lights guided her through the mudroom, through the large kitchen and into the front hall.

Here everything changed. Every bit of floor space, with the exception of a narrow path that wound through the mansion's halls and stairways, was filled from floor to ceiling with boxes of all sizes and flavors except cardboard. Cardboard was a poor material for holding worries and ills.

There were wooden boxes of every size and shape, carved and plain, adorned and unadorned, painted and unpainted. There were boxes made of brass, of silver, stainless steel, galvanized metal, tin, and iron. Boxes of precious jade, celadon, bakelite, Chinese enamel, paper maché. The variety and quantity boggled Pandora's brain.

Her female ancestors had been slaving to atone for the original Pandora's carelessness almost since recorded history began. How many of their homes existed around the globe like this one, filled from basement (or dungeon) to ceiling with boxes of worries?

The Pandora women were the ultimate hoarders. But instead of hoarding normal stuff like normal people did—toilet paper, coffee, paper, clothing, books, shoes, clocks—they hoarded something intangible, something that had no substance but possessed the power to affect billions of people.

No wonder she couldn't find a mate, reflected Pandora as she slipped the newest filled wooden box of worries onto the top of a pile. She took a moment to adjust the pile so it wouldn't crash over, then made her way back to the kitchen, the only room in the house that had yet to be filled.

Pandora had grown up in the kitchen. By the time she was born most of the mansion had already been filled with boxes. Her great-great-great-great grandmother had migrated to America from Greece and married Warren Jones in the early 1800s. She had then immediately set to work building boxes, and began to methodically fill the attic rooms with the worries she collected each night.

Subsequent generations of Pandoras filled each room, and then each floor, until Pandora and her mother, also named Pandora, were forced to move into the kitchen.

She didn't mind living in the kitchen. She loved the old red Aga stove imported from England decades before, a stove that kept the kitchen warm and homey, and the pale, limestone fireplace at the opposite end with a sofa and two deep, leather easy chairs placed to capture the fire's heat on cold winter days.

She loved to sit at the old scarred farm table and drink her tea from a thick pottery mug while she looked out the large rear-facing windows.

Somewhere under all the boxes in the fancy dining room with its punched tin ceiling and artist painted walls was a formal cherry dining set and a matching cherry buffet filled with the family's best china and silver.

She had no idea when the dining table had last been used. Her mother had pointed out the dining room doorway to Pandora once, but by then the room was stuffed with boxes and the hall path had bypassed it so she'd never actually stepped foot in there.

She stored her meager wardrobe in a lower section of an old, marred walnut buffet that rose to the ceiling and held what were once the servant's dishes, mixing bowls, and what books had been rescued before the library's shelves had been blocked with boxes.

Pandora set the tea kettle on the Aga to heat and slipped into her favorite blue and white striped flannel pajamas and heavy wool socks. It took only minutes to heat the water for her favorite peppermint tea.

She carried the steaming mug to one of the leather chairs and sank gracefully into it. Staring into the low-burning fire, inhaling the fragrant scent wafting from the mug, she contemplated her life. It was something she found herself doing too often lately.

Thirty years old. The house was nearly filled. She had no marriage prospects, not even someone she could use to impregnate her and then discard. She had no friends and no family left in the U.S.

Where would she go next? Her mother had always told her not to worry about the future. "The future will take care of itself," was her mother's favorite answer when Pandora questioned her about money and what she should do when the house could hold no more worries.

Now her mother was gone. Pandora had one room left to fill, the room she lived in, and the family money was nearly gone as well. Her mother had not planned well, and had left Pandora with few options.

Pathetic. Her life was pathetic and she had nobody to blame but herself. And the original Pandora, of course.

With a heavy sigh, she set down her tea mug on a small table set beside the chair and picked up a fine carving chisel and the block of wood that would soon be a new box.

The set of chisels had been a gift from her grandfather to her grandmother, passed to her mother, and then to her. Their wooden handles were smooth and warm and golden brown from years of skin oils working into the grain.

She set to work, cutting away delicate slivers of wood from the intricate design she had sketched onto the block of maple. She needed to finish this next box to replace the one she would soon fill. And then make the next. And the next. Repeat the process until death.

Pandora slumped in her seat, ran her finger lightly over the partly-finished design. Two hearts, entwined, with a vine winding sinuously around the outer edge of the lid. Two hearts entwined . . . was she trying to tell herself something?

She picked up the box to hurl it into the fire but her hand refused to release it. She needed this box. And the carving was lovely. Over the years she had become quite skilled.

Her hand dropped back into her lap.

Lord she was in a mood tonight. Her life was so . . . small. Unsatisfactory. Sure, she collected people's worries and locked them away. Supposedly she made the world a better place.

So what?

Tonight she had stood outside a woman's window and watched her pace the floor with a young child in her arms. The child was running a fever and the woman didn't have the money to take a cab to the emergency room, nor did she have the money to pay for the ER visit. She had been almost sick with her worry.

The woman's worry had been so intense that it leaked from the house and filled the tiny strip of bare dirt between the house and the street.

Pandora had been drawn to it like a bee to honey.

She had gathered the worry around her hand, consolidated it, tucked it into her cape to join the others already collected that evening, and carried them home to secure in a box.

She had done this night after night without a break since she was seven years old; first with her mother, and after her mother's death, on her own, irresistibly drawn to the intense worries that nearly incapacitated people and filled their lives with misery.

Did she make a difference? It seemed there were always new worries to replace the ones she took away. There were some houses that she visited on a regular basis.

Did she actually help the people inside? Make their unhappy lives better? Or was she merely perpetuating a crazy, unobtainable dream of atonement thought up by an ancestor who should have been committed to an asylum?

Maybe she was the one who belonged in an asylum. Wasn't the definition of crazy "doing the same thing over and over and expecting a different result?"

Knock, knock, knock.

The unexpected rap on the window made Pandora jump. She turned her head and saw her neighbor's face pressed against the glass.

"Just what I need," Pandora muttered, while raising a hand in acknowledgement. She set down her tools and made her way to the back door, stopping briefly to light the burner under the teapot.

Mrs. Mackleworth loved her tea.

Pandora stood for a moment before opening the door, willing a smile to her face. She had nothing against Mrs. Mackleworth, even liked the old lady. Mrs. Mackleworth was a bit odd—who else would consider visiting a neighbor at three in the morning? — but she was friendly and pretty much the only person Pandora actually talked with.

Tonight however Pandora wanted to be alone with her thoughts. She wasn't in the mood to entertain. She sighed.

Unfortunately Mrs. Mackleworth did not take gentle hints. Pandora would have to be openly rude to get her to leave and rudeness wasn't in her. She knew that her neighbor would keep knocking until Pandora answered no matter how long it took.

Pandora opened the door and stepped aside as Mrs. Mackleworth swept her bulk into the mudroom.

"Good evening, Pandora, how are you?" Mrs. Mackleworth's bright, guileless eyes fastened on Pandora's face. "You look a little down, dear." She reached out and patted Pandora's slim arm with a pudgy, be-ringed hand.

Pandora had often wondered how the woman got the rings off her sausage-like fingers, and finally had decided that she didn't. It looked as if the fingers had swollen around the rings and they were now permanent adornment.

Mrs. Mackleworth's other hand busied itself with the buttons on a coat large enough to cover several average-sized women.

"I brought you something, dear. A young lady shouldn't be alone the way you are, so I brought you a companion."

"Oh, Mrs. Mackleworth, that's very thoughtful of you but no thank you." What on earth could her neighbor have hiding in her coat? Pandora suppressed a shudder. "I can't possibly accept—"

Before should finish the sentence Mrs. Mackleworth succeeded in removing her coat and hung it on a hook. She reached into an inside pocket and removed a tiny, black kitten. It was the smallest kitten Pandora had ever seen.

"Oh! It's so tiny! Are you sure it should be away from its mother?" Pandora cupped the mewling kitten in her hands and felt a warm rush of pleasure. The animal weighed next to nothing, his fur stood on end, and he held his tail stiff as a bottle brush. He was not happy at the moment.

It was his eyes that trapped her—smokey gray and huge in his tiny, triangular face. She felt a tug on her heart and cuddled the kitten under her chin.

"How about a cup of tea, dear?" Mrs. Mackleworth pulled an ornate red and white Chinese enamel tin from another pocket and headed into the kitchen without waiting for Pandora. She busied herself with the teapot and water, carried two mugs to the fireplace, and took the chair next to Pandora's carving chair.

"I see you're working on another box." She set one mug on the table next to Pandora's chair and ran a chubby finger lightly over the half-finished carving. "It's beautiful, dear. What *do* you do with them all? Yes, the kitten is tiny. He was the runt of the litter. Found them under the back steps. No one wanted him, so I thought of you all alone in this great big house."

Pandora said nothing. She had grown used to her neighbor's habit of quickly shifting topics and knew to wait. Mrs. Mackleworth's dark eyes watched with approval as Pandora set down a small dish of milk for the kitten and placed him on the floor next to it.

"I brought over a couple cans of food as well to get you started," she continued. "You'll have to get him some of that dry kibble stuff, of course. Now tell me, dear, what's got you down?"

She settled her bulk in her chair and sipped from her mug. "Drink your tea, dear. It's a special blend I made up just for you."

Pandora looked at her neighbor and groaned silently. She knew Mrs. Mackleworth meant well, but she simply wasn't used to sharing her inner thoughts and feelings with others.

She picked up the mug of tea to stall, and held it under her nose. Floral notes with an underlying exotic spice teased her nose. She took a cautious sip. It was surprisingly good.

Pandora sipped at her tea, saying nothing as she watched the kitten finish the milk, then scooped him up and settled back into her chair. The kitten plopped into the slight valley of her lap and promptly went to sleep.

"Mrs. Mackleworth, I appreciate the kitten, but there's nothing wrong with me. I'm fine, really."

Her neighbor said nothing, merely watched her, and waited. Her outfit—bright purple pantsuit, rose-colored blouse, thick ropes of gold chain hanging over her large bosom, and bangled wrists—looked more suited for a fortune-teller's circus tent than a social visit.

Amethyst drop earrings caught the firelight and twinkled at her large ear lobes. Every finger wore a heavy, ornate ring.

Pandora wondered if the woman ever dressed down. Despite her great size, she had never seen Mrs. Mackleworth in the leisure wear—loose sweats—that the large-bodied tend to favor.

Every time Pandora saw her she was dressed as if she were on her way to a public engagement. Her colorful outfits were all top quality and coordinated and always accessorized with ample jewelry that appeared to be real. The only thing out of place were her neighbor's shoes. Mrs. Mackleworth wore Birkenstock sandals with everything.

Pandora checked out the purple leather sandals (were they custom-made?) and saw that her neighbor had painted her toenails purple to match the pantsuit, with small rose flowers to match the blouse painted on the center of each big toenail.

She tried to picture Mrs. Mackleworth painting her toes and failed. Could she even reach them around her bulk? she wondered.

"Mrs. Mackleworth, I appreciate your concern, but—"

"I used to visit with your mother you know, after her mother died. She had a bit of a rough patch before she met your father."

Pandora blinked in surprise. "You knew my mother?"

Mrs. Mackleworth chuckled, a deep, throaty sound. "Well of course, dear. I knew your mother and also your grandmother. I've lived next door for a great many years."

Pandora almost dropped her mug. "How can that be? The Pandora women live a long time. I mean . . . I don't understand," she finished lamely.

Her neighbor's red-painted lips spread in a wide smile. "Well, of course you understand. Think about it, dear. How can I possible have known your grandmother . . . unless I am like you, and not entirely mortal?"

CHAPTER 4

THE BROTHER'S date with the girls went as their dates usually did. The girls dressed to entice and looked at the brothers with worshipful eyes. The redhead, Delia, showed up in a short, body-skimming, emerald green dress that left nothing to the imagination.

They dined and gyrated on the dance floor until the small hours of the morning. Delia rubbed her curvy body all over Zee, giggling and tossing her hair, letting him know he could do with her as he wished.

When Pauli took his blonde back to their house to finish the night, Zee took the redhead home to her apartment.

She was not happy with the way her evening had ended and let Zee know about her feelings as she flounced out of the cab and stormed up the walk to her apartment. Just before slamming her apartment door in Zee's face, she stuck her hand out and flipped Zee the bird.

"Nice girl," the cab driver commented, a bemused expression on his face, when Zee returned to the vehicle.

Zee shrugged and settled into the back seat. The cab was clean and well-maintained, the leather seats whole and supple:

one of the advantages of living in a pricey zip code—better quality everything.

"I think the lovely lady had another ending in mind for her evening," the driver continued, watching Zee in the rear view mirror. "I must say, I'm a little shocked you didn't oblige her. Fine body on that one."

"She bored me." And what was up with that? wondered Zee. Since when did he get bored with a beautiful woman? They all had something to offer. And the driver was right, this one had a body better than any amusement park.

But Zee hadn't felt the slightest need to avail himself of what Delia had blatantly offered him. In fact, if he was going to be honest with himself, he hadn't felt the slightest tug of attraction for either of the women tonight.

He looked out the cab window at the walled estates with their security lights and perfectly manicured lawns and dark windows. Everything felt so . . . sterile, so much the same.

Everyone lived in big, gated houses, wore the same designer clothes and ate at the same current hot spots and attended the same events that all ran together into one big, fat, nothing.

What was *wrong* with him? A small burst of panic clenched in his belly. This life was all he knew. He had been raised in it, embraced it, played his role well. Until today.

The cab stopped at the ornate cast iron gates to the house Zee rented with his brother. He paid the driver, gave him a generous tip and climbed out of the cab.

Zee waited until the cab's red taillights winked on at the end of the road, then turned and drove off before he keyed his code into the security panel built into the rock wall to the left of the gates.

The house, built of wood, stone, and glass in the 1920s for a now-forgotten film star, was dark but for a dim flicker of candlelight in the top northeast corner that was Pauli's room. No mistaking what was going on up there.

Zee stared at the window for a long moment, then slipped off his Italian leather loafers and silk socks and walked across the damp lawn. The dewed grass felt cool and refreshing on his bare feet. He circled the far side of the house and made his way to the private beach in front.

The tide was out, the sand damp and firm. Green phosphorescence tinged the top of each small wave as it raced to shore and spent itself on the beach. Overhead the Milky Way dazzled. The rush of water on the beach was the only sound.

Zee stuffed his socks into the loafers and set them on the edge of the dock, then pulled off his polo shirt. Clad only in khaki shorts that rode low on his hips he ran slowly down the beach, setting his pace to a mindless jog.

"What happened to you last night?" Pauli had just returned from dropping his overnight guest off at her apartment. He was still ticked off about the lambasting he had been forced to endure from his date's redheaded roommate.

"You really pissed Delia off, you know. She was expecting to climb aboard the Zee-train and you take her home instead? I don't get you, bro. You never turn down a pretty woman. What gives?"

Pauli poured himself a mug of coffee and tried to hide his worry. On a normal morning following a double date, the brothers would be sharing breakfast with the girls, and depending on how well they liked them, possibly setting up another date for the coming evening.

Zee and Pauli were close. They did nearly everything together and that included their dating. Last night had been a glaring anomaly and it made Pauli uneasy. He looked at the purple shadows under Zee's eyes and wondered if his brother was ill.

Ignoring Pauli's poorly hidden worry, Zee zipped his duffle and slung it over his shoulder without answering. He finished his buttered sesame bagel in two bites and headed for the front door.

"Zee? What's wrong with you?" Pauli followed and grabbed at his brother's arm, suddenly determined to get some answers. Something was bothering Zee and he needed to know what it was.

Zee stopped and turned, scowled at his younger sibling. "I think Father did something to me yesterday when he called me about that errand of his. I haven't felt like myself since I talked with him. I have a feeling he didn't want me to get distracted so he put some whammy-spell on me. It's the only explanation I can come up with."

Pauli's eyes got large and round. "Oh shit. If the old man whammied you you're sunk."

The brothers stared at each other glumly. Their father pretty much left them alone to live their lives as they saw fit, but when he did interfere, he interfered in a big way. If he wanted Zee to remain focused on the errand, then he wouldn't think twice about making women unattractive to his eldest son.

"Maybe he'll ease up when he sees that you're working on the errand." Pauli hesitated. "Just what is this mysterious errand anyway? You never said."

Zee shrugged. "He wants me to find somebody. I don't know why he's being so mysterious about it. He won't tell me more until I find some woman. I don't know if I'm supposed to bring her to him or what. I guess I'll find out once I locate her."

Outside, sunshine glinted off his new Harley. Custom painted burgundy and black with chrome highlights, the bike was a work of art.

A small thrill zapped through Zee and lightened his mood a

little. He appreciated sleek rides that moved fast. His new bike was the sleekest and fastest new model on the road.

Zee strapped his duffle onto the back of his seat and picked up his helmet. Instead of putting it on, he walked back to Pauli and gave him a brotherly hug.

"I'll be fine, stop worrying. You're worse than Mother. I'm not coming back here after I finish Dad's errand. I need a change of scenery. I'm thinking some striped bass fishing off New England might be fun. Join me if you want."

He strapped on his helmet and mounted his bike. One kick and she started. The sound of the engine shattered the quiet morning. Zee reveled in the power vibrating between his legs. With a grin and a wave he roared down the driveway, through the gates, and east to the Mississippi River.

CHAPTER 5

ALTHOUGH THE NOTION of getting a pet had never crossed Pandora's mind, she soon got used to having the tiny kitten underfoot. She named him Squirt, in honor of his size and prayed he wouldn't grow so large that the name no longer fit.

She hated when names didn't fit. Like giant men named Tiny. Or bald men called Curly. She didn't get the ironic name thing. Things should be called what they were so there could be no confusion.

For his part, the kitten behaved as if he'd been born in the mansion. He skittered around the kitchen on his tiny feet, his short bristly pencil of a tail standing stiff as he chased dust bunnies and the catnip mouse Pandora bought for him.

When he tired he mewed to be picked up and cuddled, and invariably fell asleep in her lap, his tiny voice box rasping his pleasure.

She had never cuddled with a live creature before the kitten. There was something soothing about stroking its soft fur and listening to the rattle of its purred response.

She had baked a batch of snickerdoodles and brought them to

Mrs. Mackleworth to thank her for the gift but her neighbor hadn't been home.

She handed the cookies to a woman she assumed was the housekeeper with a message, although she wasn't sure the house-keeper—an ancient, gray-haired stick of a woman who looked like a slight gust of air could knock her over—understood English. The housekeeper had nodded and taken the cookies with a gap-toothed smile and shut the door in Pandora's face.

The first night that Pandora had to leave the kitten, she padded a high-sided cardboard box with an old towel and set the kitten inside until she could return for him.

But when she finished the night's collection of worries and hurried back to the house, she found Squirt sitting on the back stoop, mewling piteously.

"How did you get out here, little fella?" she asked as she picked up the shivering kitten and tucked him inside her cape. She dumped the night's worries into the newly finished box and hung up her cape, snugging the still-mewling kitten under her chin. If she didn't know better she would swear he was berating her for leaving him behind.

When he escaped every container she put him in for three nights straight and sat crying for her on the back stoop, she decided to take the kitten with her. She had plenty of pockets in her cape and he weighed next to nothing, certainly no more than a worry.

The next night Pandora set out with Squirt tucked safely against her chest. She could feel him rumble while he slept and was glad she had brought him. He made her feel less alone as she scoured the small city for the worst of the worries.

Finding the worst of the worries was one of the biggest issues with her job. People had so many things to worry about that it would have been an impossible task to gather and box them all, so her mother had taught her to grade the worries she found on a scale of one through five, and only gather the fives.

A one worry would be something like getting a good parking space downtown. Or a student worrying about an upcoming exam. Unless failing the exam meant expulsion from school, then the worry would be rated higher—a three or four maybe, depending on what expulsion meant to the student.

A five would be a poor mother wondering how to feed her children, or how to pay for medicine for a sick child. Anything involving children usually fell into a four or a five.

Because she had to be selective about the worries she gathered, Pandora spent most of the night walking through neighborhoods and noting the fives.

She hated that the same poor neighborhoods were the ones she pulled from night after night. Hated that life mostly didn't improve for the people who lived in the small, run-down houses with their dirt yards and trash-lined streets.

Gathering the worst of their worries didn't seem to be helping them, but she didn't know what else she could do. She had been raised and groomed to collect worries, to try to atone for the great wrong that the original Pandora had unleashed on the world.

It was all she knew. That and box-making.

After scouting the city, Pandora returned to gather the worst of the category five worries at the end of each work shift, always keeping her eyes open for any that might rate more heartbreaking on her small scale.

A week after Mrs. Mackleworth dropped off the kitten, Pandora and Squirt walked along the Mississippi River in Riverside Park. Their night's scouting had finished early and she felt depressed. Finishing early was never a good thing as it meant there were far too many people with category five worries.

Rather than look for more, Pandora had decided to visit the park until it was time to complete her task.

She loved Riverside Park. In operation since 1911, it boasted large old trees, lots of green space, and a long, paved walkway along the river's edge with benches for day visitors to sit and watch the riverboats and various birds that used the river.

Although night's darkness hid most of the park's amenities, Pandora found it peaceful and beautiful. She walked on the grass edge of the walkway, reveling in the feel of ground instead of concrete beneath her feet, and wondered what it would feel like to walk along a beach, to feel the sand give beneath her bare feet.

A large tugboat pushed three massive barges in the middle of the channel, its powerful engines chugging, its red and green running lights clear in the cool night air. The barges were lined end-to-end and rode low in the water, heavy with grain that had wintered in large silos up river.

The *Mississippi Queen*, resting from her daily runs carrying tourists on the river, sat at her mooring for the night, her paddle-wheel gleaming in the moonlight. Brown bats plied the air over the water, their wingbeats fast as they swooped and dived on newly hatched insects.

The kitten insisted on being set down to explore so Pandora sat on a bench to keep an eye on him. Not far down river soared the two big blue bridges that connected La Crosse to Pettibone Island, where the river channel narrowed and she could see across to the island's public beach.

The small beach was empty this time of night of course, as was the park, except for the occasional group of drunk and rowdy college students taking a detour on their way home from the bars that peppered the historic district of downtown La Crosse.

One such group, all young men, walked down to the water

near Pandora's bench and dared each other to jump in. They never noticed the still, dark figure sitting nearby.

Since snow melt and melting ice was still making its way from the headwaters into the river, Pandora knew that death by hypothermia was a real threat.

She prayed none of the men were foolish enough or drunk enough to try a swim. Every year the city lost a student or two who tried to swim the great river while inebriated. The senseless waste of a life always saddened her. Death by stupidity made her angry.

The group of college boys eventually left without dipping a toe into the water and Pandora relaxed. Squirt had tired of his explorations and curled up on her boot. She leaned down and picked him up, cupping him in both hands, than tucked him inside her cloak. It was time to finish her night's work.

Pandora cut away from the river and across the green. High above her, the occasional truck crossed the west bound bridge. A car flew over the bridge heading for Minnesota, salsa music blaring.

Beneath it she heard the dull thrum of a powerful engine.

She stopped and cocked her head to better hear the engine. The salsa music faded, and she realized the vehicle with the powerful engine was heading east toward La Crosse on the one-way bridge farthest from where she stood.

Smooth and deep, the engine's power reached into her body and made her blood hum. It revved, and she swore she revved with it.

She followed the sound with her ears, mentally picturing it's path. When it reached Fourth Street, a one way through down-town, it turned and headed north. Then it turned east and was gone.

Pandora took a deep breath and shook herself. What sort of

vehicle could crawl under a woman's skin like that? It felt as if the thrum of that engine had reached out and mesmerized her.

She must be tired. It was definitely time to finish her work and go home. She put the hypnotic engine out of her mind and headed to her first worry pick-up.

CHAPTER 6

A WEEK after leaving southern California, Zee crossed a big blue bridge that arched high above the Mississippi River. The bridge soared over the river, high enough for any size boat or ship to pass under it, even during flood stage.

Far beneath him he spotted a tugboat pushing long, flat barges, the reflections of it's red and green lights twinkling on the river's smooth surface.

He almost stopped to get a better look, but a vehicle parked in the breakdown lane would attract the police and he didn't feel like explaining himself at three in the morning. It was well known that cops didn't look upon strangers with a friendly eye at this hour.

He had taken his time getting to La Crosse. The drive through the desert southwest had been fun, the canyon lands of southern Utah and the Rocky Mountains spectacular.

The Grand Canyon had reminded him of his father and uncles, the way they liked to hurl thunderbolts when they got angry. They weren't supposed to actually strike anything—the bolts were mostly for show, a way to let lesser beings know they were displeased—but sometimes shit happened. He wondered if the canyon had been born from a careless bolt.

It had been a long day, starting west of Mount Rushmore, where he had taken the time to stop and view the giant faces with amused interest. The carved heads reminded him of the giant statues of Egypt and India and other places where the people liked to honor their gods with monstrous-sized images in their imagined likeness.

He had crossed two entire states and part of Wyoming in a single long day. Two *big* states in one long haul, with only short breaks for food and fuel. South Dakota, from western mountains to hills to flatland, angling southeast into the southern end of Minnesota—unrelieved flat land—until he reached the high bluffs that ran along the eastern edge of the state.

It had been like riding through an ocean of bare ground as the crop fields had yet to be planted. Mile after mile of flat brown dirt, relieved at intervals with farm buildings and their small plantings of trees to stop the prairie's relentless wind.

Fortunately the wind had been at his back because it had blown all day. How did people live here? he wondered as he eyed the barren land. He thought of the Pacific Ocean with its eerie phosphorescence, the waves crashing off the Hawaiian island chain, the warm waters off Tahiti.

Three quarters of the Earth was covered in water. He couldn't imagine choosing to live away from it, and yet apparently people did.

It all came down to what a person was used to, he guessed. He needed to be near water, preferably a large and salty body of water.

He'd been happy to get through the prairie and reach the bluffs. They contained both edges of the Mississippi River: Wisconsin to the east and Minnesota to the west.

Zee could see their dark shadows from the bridge and made a

note to look for a river drive during the daylight hours. He needed a water fix and the river would have to do. At least it was a big river.

But right now, he needed to find a shower and a bed. Tomorrow would be soon enough to contact his father and find out why he was here.

CHAPTER 7

THE NEXT NIGHT Pandora stood in the small bare patch of dirt that passed for a yard in the poor neighborhood. Blaring music, engines revving, a loud argument from two houses down filled the air. Where there should have been peace and quiet with families tucked into bed, there was the discord of poverty and unfulfilled dreams.

She hated that she was here again. No matter how many worries she pulled from this house there always seemed to be more waiting to take their place.

At least tonight it wasn't the baby, she saw with relief. Despite the noise, the baby slept quietly in an old worn crib that had been squeezed into a small bedroom shared with three other siblings.

Pandora felt almost guilty that she lived alone in a huge mansion, a mansion where one bedroom could easily hold this entire house including the yard, with plenty of space to spare.

No need to feel bad, she told herself. She may live in one of the largest house in La Crosse, but she only lived in one room of it.

She forced the guilt from her mind and watched the scene inside the small house through badly worn but clean curtains. It was the curtains that got to her every time she came here. Washed so many times they were almost transparent, they were little more than rags, but the mother kept them clean, just like the rest of the house.

She took care of what little she had.

Because of that caring, Pandora visited her nearly every night to see if she could lighten the woman's burden by carrying away a worry.

Tonight the mother was having a serious talk with her oldest boy, a boy of about ten or eleven, a boy who had come home only moments before at a little after three in the morning.

Pandora knew where he'd been. She had seen him earlier with a gang of boys ranging in age from eight to seventeen. They were peering in windows, the older boys lifting the young ones to their shoulders to see into the ones that were too high.

And why would they be looking into windows at this time of night? She had a good idea, especially when she saw a young boy boosted through a small window of a well-kept house. He unlocked the back door and the oldest of the gang slipped inside, then slipped out several minutes later with his pockets filled to bursting and a small stuffed bag over his shoulder.

Because of what she saw every night, Pandora knew how difficult life was for boys like the one she watched now. How alluring the street gangs could be. The gangs gave kids like this one a sense of belonging. A way to make money. A way to hide the mantle of poverty that labeled a person "loser" even when being poor wasn't their fault.

The mother knew where her son had been as well. She was angry, her small, red-knuckled hands fisted at her side while she lectured her son and told him to have some pride, don't fall prey to those who would use him until he was of no use.

The son glared at his mother defiantly, told her she had no right to stop him from making a better life for himself, and stormed off to the bedroom filled with his younger brothers and sisters.

Pandora watched as the woman's shoulders drooped, her hands unfisted at her side. Tears streamed down her face when she turned toward the window.

Pandora reached up and snagged the worry, wrapped it into a tight coil and dropped it into a pocket. She would add watching out for the boy to her nightly search, she decided. Maybe she could help keep one life from spiraling out of control.

She reached into her cape, ran a fingertip down Squirt's triangular face, then left the house's small dirt patch to finish the night's collection.

While she worked her thoughts kept returning to the boy. He needed help, probably more help than his mother or Pandora could give him. He needed something positive in his life, a true role model, someone else who cared.

His mother did her best by her children, but at the moment she wasn't enough. The lure of the thieving gangs and what masqueraded as easy money was too strong for the boy to resist.

Pandora worried over the problem as she made her way home. She hadn't stopped outside the female student's apartment since Mrs. Macklworth gave her Squirt, but tonight something drew her attention and made her slip into the shadows to watch.

As usual, the pretty blonde was entertaining. Her guests this evening included another pretty blond and two men.

It was the men who drew Pandora's attention. To be more precise, it was one of the men who caught—and held her attention. She couldn't look away from him.

He dominated the room, and both women hung onto him while the other male, an average-looking Joe dressed in jeans and a snug tee shirt, stood to the side looking a little put-out.

Pandora didn't blame him. The man currently sandwiched

between the two blondes had to be the most beautiful man she had ever seen.

Truly, the most beautiful. Eye candy that made her heart leap in her chest.

He stood tall, about six-two she judged, broad shoulders filling a black and burgundy long-sleeved tee that hugged his torso like an expensive glove. His shoulders tapered to a trim waist, with a nice tight butt and long, muscled legs wrapped in supple black leather.

He stood in profile to the window, his wavy black hair just grazing his shoulders. He had a strong nose and chin, full lips and . . . he turned his head and looked at the window, seemed to stare right into Pandora's eyes.

The breath left her body. Even from where she stood she could see that his eyes were a beautiful, smoky gray and thickly lashed. Although she knew she stood hidden, the man's eyes seemed to lock onto her.

Pandora's heart stuttered in her chest, until the apartment blonde shook the man's arm and rubbed against him suggestively, drawing his attention away from the window.

The spell broken, Pandora sucked in a lungful of air and hurried across the parking lot to the narrow gap in the thick hedge that separated the lot from her back yard. She pushed through it and ran across the large yard without checking as she usually did.

Her hands shook as she unlocked her back door.

Once inside she whipped off her cape, set Squirt on the floor, and dumped the night's worries into the waiting box. Squirt mewed and darted into the kitchen while Pandora removed her worn boots and pulled on thick wool socks.

She poured kibble into Squirt's bowl and put on the kettle for herself. While she was pouring the tea water a knock sounded on the back door. Pandora started and splashed hot water on the old tiled counter. Had he followed her?

No, of course not. She was being foolish.

"Honestly, Pandora. Pull yourself together. It's only your neighbor." She wiped up the spilled water and walked back to the mudroom. Despite knowing better, a small part of her hoped that the leather clad man would be standing there when she opened the door.

What would she do if he came to her door, she wondered. Act nonchalant, as if she had been expecting him? Or shriek and throw herself into his arms?

Probably neither, she decided. She'd play the coward and refuse to open the door. Thoroughly disgusted with herself, Pandora threw open the door.

"Hi, Mrs. Mackleworth." Glad for the company, Pandora stepped back and gestured for her neighbor to enter. "I was just making some tea. Come on in. Can I get you a cup?"

"That would be grand, dear. I just stopped by to see how you and the kitten are getting along." Mrs. Mackleworth whipped off her voluminous brown wool cloak and hung it on a hook next to Pandora's. She pulled a bag of dried herb from one of its many pockets.

"I brought some extra tea in case you're getting low."

Pandora bit back a smile as she eyed Mrs. Mackleworth's outfit. Tonight the pantsuit was a deep, eggplant purple, her blouse a bright lime green. The Birkenstocks matched the pantsuit and she dripped in her usual abundance of jewelry.

She looked like a new species of peacock next to Pandora's worn blue jeans and faded blue long-sleeve tee.

Mrs. Mackleworth was just the diversion she needed.

The two women settled in front of the fire with their mugs of tea like old friends. Squirt clawed his way up Mrs. Mackleworth's leg onto her ample lap.

"How are you, Mrs Mackleworth? Did you get the Snicker-doodles I brought over? I left them with your housekeeper."

"Call me Mackey, dear. Everyone else does." Mrs. Mackleworth patted her round belly and smiled broadly. "The cookies were delish. Thank you. It was a thoughtful gesture. I see the kitten has settled in. Have you named him yet?"

"I call him Squirt because of his size. I'm not sure it's official. I'll have to see how much he grows. He's great company, thank you for bringing him to me, Mrs . . . Mackey."

Her neighbor beamed. "You're very welcome, dear. Now tell me, how are you doing?"

Pandora hesitated. She didn't know how much of her life she could share with the neighbor. How much did the old woman know about Pandora herself, her mother, her grandmother?

Mackey smiled over her tea mug, seemed to read Pandora's mind. She reached across and patted Pandora's hand.

"I know all about you, dear. Not to worry—little pun there, get it?— I know how to keep a secret. Are some of the worries getting to you?"

Much to Pandora's embarrassment, tears sprang to her eyes. She hadn't had anyone to talk with about her work since her mother had died ten years earlier. She dashed the tears away with the back of her hand.

"There's this one house that draws me back every night. I can't seem to stay away. The woman who lives there—she's a single parent and she has her hands full with five children. She tries so hard, but there always seems to be something dragging her down. Tonight it was her oldest child, a boy about ten or eleven, who's joined one of the city's thieving gangs."

Pandora told her neighbor, who turned out to be a surprisingly good listener, all about the woman and her family, about her own loneliness, and finally about her inability to find a suitable mate so she could have a child and keep the family legacy alive.

Once the floodgates opened there had been no holding back.

"Phew," she ended on a shaky breath. "I didn't mean to unload all of that on you. I'm so sorry." Embarrassed, she wiped more tears from her face and puffed out her cheeks. "I didn't realize I had so much bottled up."

"Don't you worry about me none, dearie. I can bear it. You've been carrying a heavy load all by yourself since your mother passed, gods rest her soul. You've a good heart, Pandora. Don't give up on finding love."

"I saw a man in a student's apartment tonight on my way home." Pandora didn't know why she was bringing this up, but now that she had started talking she couldn't seem to stop.

"He must be the most beautiful man I've ever seen. This student, I don't know her name, she has different guys over nearly every night. Sometimes I see the same ones, but mostly she plays the field. She's pretty enough, I guess, but I don't know how she does it. She doesn't seem to have any problem attracting all these men. I can't even attract one."

Squirt decided he'd had enough of Mackey's lap and tried to leap across to Pandora's but didn't quite make it. He clung to the side of her calf and mewed indignantly.

Pandora laughed and nudged him up, glad for the diversion. It felt odd to be sharing her thoughts and feelings with a woman she didn't know very well.

"Look at it from another perspective," Mackey said. "This student has no one special. The men don't stick. Don't waste any envy on her, Pandora. She's worse off than you are."

Pandora frowned. "How do you figure she's worse off? She has *men. Men.* Warm human beings. I have a tiny kitten."

"Well, for starters think of the energy she's expending entertaining these men night after night. She's frittering away her life, and eventually she'll just fade away, like smoke. She won't know who she is anymore and one day she'll have nothing left to give because she's giving it all away and not getting anything in return."

"Huh. I never looked at it that way." Pandora's mood lightened a little and she grinned at her neighbor. "Still, I'd like to fritter some energy on the guy she had there tonight. Hubba-hubba, manliest of men on the he-could-be-a-god scale."

A gleam came into Mackey's eyes. "Is that so? I wouldn't mind seeing a young man like that. Even us old ladies like to feel our engines rev now and then."

They both laughed at that and Mackey left shortly after. Pandora felt much lighter than she'd felt in a long time, years really, when she sat down to work on the newest box.

CHAPTER 8

Zee was not happy about being stuck in a podunk place like La Crosse, Wisconsin. Every time he called home to speak with his father about *why* he was there, his father was unavailable. Out with the uncles, tending to business, celebrating at a feast in his honor. And his mother refused to intervene.

If the errand was so bloody unimportant, why had he insisted that Zee leave California immediately?

The temptation to blow his father off was strong, but Zee knew that if he left La Crosse before completing his task there'd be hell to pay. Literally. He'd be punished with an extended visit to his Uncle Hades—a fate he and his brothers worked hard to avoid.

To pass the time while he waited for his father to get back to him, Zee did what he did in any new place. He checked out the lay of the land, both geographically and socially.

The La Crosse area possessed several good rides for a motor bike. He drove the roads hugging the river on the Minnesota side and the Wisconsin side. Steep bluffs edged the roads in both states, with the wide, sparkling river, dotted with green islands and alive with bird life, sandwiched in between.

He visited Effigy Mounds park and hiked to the top of the bluffs, marveled at the great river dividing the land, enjoying the majestic beauty and wildness of it.

He was surprised to learn that the upper Mississippi River was nothing like its southern end where the water became a slow moving, unappetizing, brown sludge. The upper river was clean and vibrant with wildlife that inhabited not only the river but the sky and land around it.

He explored the dirt roads that wound deep into the bluff valleys, found a mix of beautiful farms, geodesic domes and old limestone barns and farmhouses that reminded him of Greece and Italy.

He was delighted to learn that La Crosse had much to offer a young man, at least ordinary young men. Two colleges and two large medical facilities attracted a bounty of young women who came either for an education or for work. And although the small city was a mere infant compared to the ancient towns in Europe, it was attractive in its own way.

All that getting-to-know-the-place took Zee four days. When he still couldn't reach his father and his mother refused to speak with him he resigned himself to being stuck in middle America for a while.

He found a small but charming house to rent in a passable neighborhood on the the eastern edge of town and called his brother Pauli to join him. If he was going to be stuck there until his father had time to lay out the rest of his errand, he might as well have his brother to play with.

Pauli flew in, took one look at the town and the small house Zee had rented, patted his brother on the shoulder, and flew back out on the first plane he could catch.

"Can't do it, Zee. Sorry," he said, with a grin that didn't look sorry at all. "I need more stimulation than this place has to offer. Dad sent you here, not me, so I'm free to leave. I'm headed to

Monte Carlo, see if I can drum up some action there. I wouldn't mind picking up a boat and doing a little racing. Look me up when you're finished with your errand."

Zee grumbled about lack of brotherly love and loyalty but drove Pauli back to the airport, all the while wishing he could get on the plane with him.

After waving a still-grinning Pauli off, he went back to the house, sat for less than a minute, and went back out to look for a bicycle to buy. He'd noticed that La Crosse was a bike-friendly town, and it was a good way to get around.

Plus the exercise might help burn off some of his building frustration while he waited for his father to get back to him. There was also the fact that while he loved his Harley, sometimes a man wanted to be more subtle. It was hard to be subtle on a powerful machine like the Harley.

He settled on a sleek black hybrid bike with fat nobby tires that could handle woods trails and city streets. The owner of the bike shop agreed to add burgundy accents to the frame and a deal was struck.

The novelty of riding a bicycle did help take some of the edge off Zee's mood. Zee and his brothers had been raised to be physical; developing strong muscles and stamina through foot races, swimming, riding, strength competitions, weaponry use—they had competed against each other in every sport invented.

A day without exercise left Zee feeling like a caged animal.

Daylight hours he rode the off-road bike trails. Nights he tooled around the city, getting to know its nooks and crannies, his strong thighs pumping the pedals until the wheel spokes blurred and the tires hummed.

It was on one of these night rides that he ran into Eleanor, a curvy blonde sitting on her front stoop waiting for her friends. She invited Zee in and he accepted.

The friends turned out to be a couple, an average guy named

David, and his slightly above average blonde girlfriend Susie. Although Zee did his best to engage David in conversation, the girls fawned all over him and made it difficult.

He stood in Eleanor's small living room, a girl on either side, music blasting, and wondered what he was doing there. He hadn't been with a woman since southern California and now he had two who were practically drooling on him. Yet he felt nothing. Not the slightest twinge of desire.

It wasn't that the girls weren't attractive, they were. They were a little young for his taste, both students, and a little naive in their limited middle-America upbringing, but they were nice enough.

Eleanor's apartment was decorated with used furniture and bright cotton throws to disguise their age and wear. She had tacked more throws onto the walls instead of hanging pictures or posters. He found that interesting.

But that was about all he found interesting, he realized. Accepting her invitation had been a mistake. He would have been happier sitting down with a beer and talking with Susie's boyfriend David.

Zee stood near the window, a girl on either arm and made up his mind to leave. But before he could say anything he felt a slight buzz in his blood. The hair on the back of his neck stirred.

He turned his head and looked out the window but saw only his reflection with the two girls hanging on him. Still, something outside was pulling on him.

Eleanor tugged on his arm and rubbed her breast against it, gave him the unmistakable come hither look. He smiled and plucked her hand from his arm, then removed Susie's hand from his other arm.

Stepping away from the girls, he walked over to where David sat staring morosely into his beer and leaned down, tapping him on the shoulder to get his attention.

"They're all yours, pal. I have to run. Nice meeting you."

David looked up and scowled at Zee. When he realized that Zee meant to leave he grinned. He jumped up and thumped Zee on the back.

"Nice meeting ya, man. Take care."

"Sure, you too. Bye, ladies." Zee raised a hand in farewell, ignored the disappointed looks on the girls' faces, and slipped out of the apartment.

Once outside, Zee didn't immediately bike away. He took the time to walk around Eleanor's building, stopping and staring in her window.

He noted the parking lot bounded by a tall, thick hedge on one long side and apartment buildings that shared the lot on the opposite side. The lot opened onto the street at one end and a dirt alley at the opposite end.

He found no one lurking in the shadows and finally left feeling a little unsettled.

Something had happened while he was standing in Eleanor's living room, he was sure of it, but he hadn't a clue what that something was. He mounted his bicycle and rode around the neighborhood and through the alleyways, taking a thorough look around.

He saw people hauling recycle bins to the curb for the next day's trash pick-up and stray dogs and cats nosing for scraps of food but nothing that buzzed for him.

Instead of heading across the river as he'd planned, Zee headed home and went to bed. Tomorrow he would harass everybody he could reach until he got hold of his father. It was time to finish this foolish errand, whatever it was, and get back to his life.

CHAPTER 9

PANDORA WAITED until her night's work was almost finished before she stopped by the woman's house. She tried to talk herself out of checking on her—it wasn't good to get attached to a worry's owner. But no matter what argument she used, she still found herself drawn to the neat little house with the bare dirt patch.

Pandora found the woman pacing the small living room and wringing her hands. The woman stopped several times and reached for the phone, then jerked her hand back and resumed her pacing.

Did one of the children need a doctor?

Pandora slipped around the side of the house, her booted feet silent in the packed dirt. In contrast to the woman's neat but dismal yard, trash blew in the yard next door. Paper cups, plastic bags, and sales flyers lay plastered against the back stoop like metal filings drawn to a magnet.

The neighboring house's windows, thick with grime, barely reflected the light thrown by a lone street lamp. A rusted grill and bicycle chained to the sagging porch finished off the decorating theme. Given the weeds that grew up through their frames,

Pandora doubted that either item had seen any use in several years.

What did the woman think when she looked through her own sparkling clean windows at such a depressing reminder of where she lived? The small hooks of attachment, already firmly in place, latched a little deeper into Pandora's heart.

She stopped beside the children's bedroom window and slowly peeped in. Two sets of bunk beds nearly filled the small room. A narrow rectangular rug, once bright red, now a faded pink, ran between the beds.

Two small bodies sprawled together in the righthand lower bunkbed, their legs entwined, one thin arm thrown across the chest of the other. A single sleeping form filled the second upper bunk.

Okay, the two kids sleeping together was easy enough to figure—the kid who slept in the top bunk had joined his brother or sister, whoever slept below. It was hard to tell if they were boys or girls. They wore faded footed pajamas and their heads were buried beneath pillows and ragged stuffed animals.

And the third kid was accounted for. That left the oldest boy and the baby. Where was the baby?

Fear fisted around Pandora's heart as she hurried across the back of the house to look into the mother's bedroom. Please don't have let anything happen to the baby, she pleaded silently. This woman already bears so much.

The fist released her heart with a whoosh of expelled breath when she saw the mother had moved the crib into her own bedroom.

The mother had taken the smaller of the two bedrooms. It held a double mattress on the floor, a short, painted dresser with a cracked mirror, and the crib.

A padded bottom stuck up in the air in the center of the crib mattress.

"Huh." The relief was so great it forced Pandora to turn around and lean against the house.

Four children accounted for. That left the oldest boy. Given the mother's worried pacing, Pandora was willing to bet the boy hadn't come home yet tonight.

"All right, Squirt, let's see if we can be a little more useful tonight and find the son." Pandora reached into her cloak and scratched between the kitten's ears. He rumbled in response.

She must touch him a hundred times a night, she mused. It felt so nice to have company while performing her lonely and mostly thankless life's work.

Pandora circled the neighborhood first, to be sure the son wasn't just hanging with his pals. She knew the gang he was hanging with worked different neighborhoods in the hopes they wouldn't get caught.

She had passed them on Winter Street on her way out last night. She figured the gang leader itched to get inside the large houses that lined Winter, but hadn't quite worked up the nerve because most of those homes were alarmed and the police frequently patrolled the neighborhood.

If a cop even spotted a gang member walking in the area they'd move them along or take them into the central station to harass them.

She shuddered to think what would happen if they broke into her place and opened the boxes filled with worries.

Don't go there Pandora, she chided herself. No one in the long line of Pandoras has ever lost a worry once it was boxed. There was no reason to think she'd be the first.

Years of walking had honed Pandora's body into a lean, muscled machine. She ate up the ground with long strides, her dark cloak flowing around her as she worked her way through the neighborhoods surrounding Winter Street. She saw only the late partiers and bar workers heading for their homes.

No gang and no sign of the woman's son.

Frustrated now, Pandora sat on a stone wall to think.

The stone wall felt cool and rough under her hands. Other than the occasional car passing by on Losey Boulevard two blocks east of where she sat, the neighborhood was asleep and quiet. A dog barked once and was silent. She smelled fresh-turned earth, most likely from the numerous flower beds that decorated the surrounding yards.

These were the homes of La Crosses's middle class working population. Mostly single family with a few student apartments sprinkled in, the neighborhoods were neat and well-tended.

Losey Boulevard was more or less the eastern boundary of the city of La Crosse, although technically the city included the narrow strip between the boulevard and Granddad's Bluff.

The bluff was nearly vertical—too vertical for building sites— so it remained unspoiled. It towered over the boulevard and the railroad track that ran at its base. A small city park had been built at the top, a park with spectacular views down the Mississippi River.

Pandora had climbed up to the park more than once, on nights when she felt too worn out to deal with her life, and let the natural beauty sooth her.

She forced her thoughts back to the problem at hand. Where was the boy? The gang had its territory—every gang had its territory—a territory they defended fiercely, a territory they wouldn't stray from and risk a fight they might not win.

Granddad's Bluff bounded the boy's gang territory to the east, the river to the west. Losey Boulevard angled diagonally from the intersection near where she sat toward the river, and would act as a southern boundary. How far north would they go?

Main Street, she decided. Two blocks north of Winter Street.

Although the largest, finest homes of the city stood on Winter Street there were many fine neighborhoods fanning out from it.

If the gang tried to take more than two blocks beyond Winter they would have to fight to defend their turf. With Main Street as a northern boundary the rival gang would also have decent pickings and confrontations would be minimalized.

Satisfied with her reasoning, Pandora got to her feet. "Okay, Squirt. We're going to take a run down Losey and see if we spot anyone."

She jogged east to the first intersection, slowed to look for cyclists, and started across. Something caught her eye, a small movement beneath a large hackberry tree. Pandora crossed silently to the corner, looking like nothing more than a shadow, and stood listening.

A small dark shadow came out of a driveway and was greeted by the taller shadow waiting under the tree.

"Give it to me," hissed the tall shadow.

Pandora watched the boy empty his pockets and hand over the stolen items. She inched closer, knowing they couldn't see her unless she wanted them to.

"All of it now, Luke, you little bastard. What'd I tell you about holding back?" The tall shadow reached out and backhanded the boy. Luke didn't cry out, and although Pandora could see tears glistening in his eyes, they didn't fall.

Tough kid, she thought. She was close enough now to see that she had found her quarry. The woman's son was named Luke. But what to do about it now that she knew where he was?

Her first instinct was to step up and make her presence known, but that would send both boys running.

She hadn't really thought this through, Pandora realized. She had only thought of finding the boy, not what to do with him once she did. And after watching the older boy strike Luke—not for the first time, she'd be willing to bet—she really wanted to see the older boy get his comeuppance.

"We'll do one more. The next house has a window cracked

open in the back. I'll boost you in and wait out here." The two boys, one tall and gangly, one small and slight disappeared down a driveway.

"Crap." Now what should she do? Sooner or later someone was going to catch the woman's son stealing and he would be arrested. The older kid would run off and get away. He wasn't the kind of person who took responsibility for his actions if he could shift the blame to someone else. That someone else would be Luke.

Pandora pursed her lips. She hated that the kid was being used. Somehow she had to put a stop to it. She heard footsteps and knew the older boy was returning to wait for Luke to steal what he could.

Without giving it much thought, she grabbed the tree branch over head and pulled herself up. She stood balanced on the branch near the trunk and waited.

As she had anticipated, the older boy walked under the tree and leaned against the trunk directly beneath her. He lit a cigarette. She watched the end glow red, smelled the acrid smoke as it rose and hit her in the face.

Damn. She hated the smell of cigarettes. She buried her nose in her cloak collar and tried to come up with a plan. Before she could decide what to do a man whipped into the driveway on a bicycle.

Three things happened almost simultaneously. Pandora saw Luke's face in the front window, the older boy tossed down his cigarette and took a step away from the tree, and Pandora flung herself out of the tree onto him.

She couldn't say why she did it. Or maybe she could. If she could delay the man on the bicycle for a few minutes then Luke could get away.

"Oomph, what the—?" The older gang boy struggled to free himself from the tangle of Pandora's cloak.

She did nothing to help him. "Help! Help me!" she shouted, since bicycle man hadn't shown up yet. She breathed a sigh of relief when he came loping around the corner of the house.

Loping was definitely the term for it she thought with a little flutter of her pulse. The man had the fluid grace of an athlete or a jungle cat. A big jungle cat. Panther, she thought. Dark and sleek and fluid and dangerous.

He stopped in front of her and reached down a hand.

"What are you doing on the ground, Miss? Are you all right?"

His voice made Pandora think of rich, dark chocolate and hot summer nights, of deep, dark caves and the power of water rushing over smooth, worn rocks.

Her mind went blank for a moment. What was she doing on the ground? Then she felt the body squirming beneath her and everything came rushing back. She had to protect the woman's son. She had to give Luke time to get out of the house.

She reached up a hand and let the man with the voice pull her to her feet. His hand felt large and warm and immensely strong wrapped around hers. A tingle shot up her arm and she yanked her hand away, then immediately missed the warmth of his.

What had he asked her? She tried to gather her scattered brain and remember. Oh yes, what was she doing there?

"I fell over this thief," she managed to squeak out. Good lord, what had happened to her voice? Feeling the need to put some space between her and the man, she took a step back.

"No you didn't," said the kid on the ground. "You fell on top—"

"Thief?" The man hauled the boy to his feet and kept a firm grip on his arm. "Were you trying to rob my house, boy?" There was no mistaking the threat in his voice. Apparently the thief recognized it too.

"Uh, n-no, absolutely not," he stuttered. "I was just taking a walk around the neighborhood and this nutcase dropped—"

Pandora couldn't let him finish. "Check his pockets. I saw him come out of your neighbor's place."

"I think I'll call the police instead. Let them deal with him." The man pulled a cell phone from a hidden pocket in his tee shirt and dialed nine-one-one, all the while keeping his grip on the thief.

Police? They'd want Pandora's name, wouldn't they? As a witness? How would she explain why she was wandering around this neighborhood at three in the morning? And where was the woman's son? Where was Luke? Had he gotten out of the house and gone home?

Oh, brother. She'd really done it now. Twenty three years she had wandered the city at night and no one, not a single soul, had ever seen her. Now not only had these two seen her, but the cops would be coming and want information that she couldn't give them.

They'd never believe that she lived in one of the largest mansions in the city. They'd think she was crazy, Pandora realized. They'd lock her up in the psychiatric ward of the one of the hospitals. And no one will ever know. She'd spend the remainder of her life there.

Dropping out of the tree onto the older thief hadn't been such a bright idea after all. She needed to get out of there before the cops showed up.

Pandora pulled her cloak around her and faded into the shadows. The man had everything under control, he didn't need her help. As for Luke, she could only hope he'd been smart enough to get out of the man's house while he had the chance.

"Hey, where'd she go?" She heard the thief's question as she hurried down the street. She moved her feet a little faster, aiming for an alley entrance between a garage and a yard surrounded by a short picket fence.

Zee tightened his grip on the thief's arm when he felt him try to squirm free.

"You! Miss!" Zee couldn't believe the woman had gotten so far away without him realizing she was gone. "Where do you think you're going?" he demanded.

Pandora turned around and looked at Zee in astonishment. "You can see me?" The man could see her? A small frisson of fear shivered down her spine.

"Well of course I can see you," Zee answered irritably. "Come back here."

"Well, that's just weird." People saw her, of course they saw her—during the day, or when she wasn't working. But once she put on her cloak and willed herself to the shadows nobody ever saw her. It didn't make her invisible really, they just didn't notice her.

"I said come back here." A hint of impatience had crept into the man's voice.

"No, no, I don't think so. I need to get home. Nice meeting you." Pandora broke into a run and cut through the alley. She half-feared the man would come after her and prayed that he had his hands full with the thief.

To her relief, she saw a squad car on the next through street. By the time he finished speaking with the cops she should be home.

But she took the shortest route at a near run, just in case.

CHAPTER 10

Zee waited impatiently for the two officers who had responded to his call to finish taking down all the information they needed. When searched, they found the kid had the pockets of his baggy cargo pants loaded with items that did not belong to him.

A thief indeed.

The thief sat handcuffed in the rear seat of the cruiser now, an angry scowl on his face. Zee answered the officer's questions with his eyes glued on the alley's entrance. The last place he'd seen the woman before she disappeared.

Disappeared in a hurry too. He couldn't help but wonder why.

"Did you notice anyone else hanging in the neighborhood when you arrived, Mr. Zee?" the older cop asked. He was tall and beefy with the sharp eyes of a cop who'd seen much during his career.

"No. Only that one." Now why had he just lied to an officer of the law? wondered Zee. Obviously the boy hadn't been working alone. The street gangs that stole usually worked these jobs in pairs: one on the inside with one left outside as a lookout.

Aw, blast me, he thought with disgust. Had the woman been

the lookout? And he'd let her get clean away. Fool. No wonder she had left in such a hurry.

Dammit, being stuck in this town was making him soft in the brain. He was usually a good judge of character, but he'd blown it on this one.

She was beautiful, Zee was pretty sure of that, although he hadn't seen much of her face beneath her hood: a strong chin, wide full mouth, the tip of a slim, straight nose. And she was soft—at least her hand was soft—but he'd felt the strength beneath that smooth skin.

A hand and a beautiful, shadowed face. That's all he'd seen of her.

Come to think about it, everything about her had seemed a little shadowy. Well, another duh. She had been standing in the shadows, and the hood of her dark cape had left her face in the shadows. Was that deliberate? What was she hiding from?

He wondered what color her hair was, how she was built beneath that huge cape she wore. And he kicked himself again. How much stolen loot had she had hidden in that cape while she stood there and pretended to be innocent?

Even though Zee hadn't seen her face he'd felt attracted to her and that had thrown him off his guard. He'd behaved like an idiot. He'd felt a buzz when he took her hand and helped her to her feet. A strong, pleasant, I'd-like-to-get-to-know-you buzz.

Although considering the dry, buzz-less spell he'd experienced the last couple months any buzz would have felt like an electric shock, no matter how small.

She'd known that he was attracted and used it to make her escape.

"That's all we need for now, Mr. Zee." The cop brought Zee's attention back to the present. "If you find anything missing when you check inside let us know."

He nodded toward the thief in the squad car. "And keep your

eyes open. This one should have a partner. Probably long gone by now, but he may come back."

"I'll keep my eyes peeled, Officer." You can bet on it, Zee added silently. He had a score to settle with the caped woman.

The officer headed for the passenger side of the squad car and stopped. "Someone will talk to your neighbors in the morning and see if they can identify the loot we found on that one," he said over the car's roof. "Maybe someone saw him with the other one."

Zee lifted a hand. "Great. Thank you, Officers. I hope you find the other one. Good-night."

He turned away and walked up his drive to his back door. Yeah, he wanted them to arrest the woman. She was a thief after all. But he didn't want her arrested until he got his hands on her and let her know that she couldn't pull the proverbial wool over his eyes and get away with it.

Thieves worked at night. Well, he'd be out there on his bike looking for her tomorrow night. And the night after that. He'd look for her every night until he found her. And once he did they'd have it out.

He may not be as powerful as his father, but he possessed power, oh yes he did. And it was high time the clever caped thief felt some of the wrath of the gods.

Knowing he had a plan and would work it until he succeeded made Zee feel better. He had purpose now, a reason to hang around La Crosse while he waited for his father to get back to him.

He entered his house and locked the door behind him, then took a quick look around. Nothing seemed to be missing. He didn't expect there would be. He hadn't lived here long enough to collect anything of value and he wore what little jewelry he owned.

"Slim pickings in this house, thieves," he said aloud. "You'll be sorry you ever tried to rob it."

<hr>

Pandora slipped through the hedge and rushed across her back yard to the mudroom door. Once again her hands were shaking so she could barely fit the key in the lock. She fumbled and dropped it, cursed at herself and tried again. It took her three tries to open the door.

She dumped the night's worries into their container and plucked Squirt from his pocket. He protested loudly and demanded to be put down. Once on the floor he continued to cry as he wound around her legs demanding to be fed.

"Aren't you vocal tonight?" Pandora scooped kibble and canned cat food into a dish. She set it next to a bowl of fresh water and watched Squirt settle down to eat.

Satisfied that he was happy, she quickly changed into her faded, blue striped flannel pajama bottoms, a long-sleeve tee, and heavy socks. Comfort clothes. Even during the worst heat of summer the stone mansion stayed cool inside. Pandora always dressed well for bed.

She brewed a cup of Mrs. Mackleworth's tea and sat beside the fire to think.

Tonight, for the first time ever, she had almost been caught. The near miss had left her feeling weak-kneed and shaky.

She had exposed herself to the thief, but that didn't worry her too much. He didn't get a look at her face and hadn't seen her walking away. By tomorrow he would think she was just a heavy shadow that fell out of a tree and landed on top of him.

But the homeowner—the man on the bicycle. He was a different story all together. He had seen her, really seen her.

She thought of the man's long, well-muscled, nearly naked,

thighs. They'd been right in front of her face as she sat on the thief. She'd had the strangest urge to lean forward and lick them. To taste his skin.

Her face flamed with heat at the thought. What was wrong with her?

The man hadn't been naked of course. It was just that his shorts did little to conceal his powerful legs.

And his hand. His hand had felt so strong and warm and rough on hers, the way a hand that does more than push computer keys feels. A working man's hand. She looked at her own hand, the one he had held, in wonder. It still tingled from his touch.

She brought it to her face and lightly stroked her cheek with the back. What would his hands feel like on other parts of her body? Heat flooded Pandora's face again.

She took a long sip of tea and willed herself to think of other things. Like Luke. How was she going to help Luke and his mother—preferably before Luke got into serious trouble?

No great ideas popped into her fuzzy brain. She would simply have to continue to keep an eye on the boy and see if an opportunity came up to speak with him. Hopefully he had gotten out of the man's house safely.

She wondered what the man's name was, what he did for a living.

And there she was again, thinking about him. Thinking about how close her face had been to that powerful chest wrapped in a tight, damp tee when he pulled her to her feet. The man had the body of a god.

Thinking about the magnificent body and face, those smoky gray eyes that she could see even in the dim glow of the street lamps . . . smoky gray eyes. . . good god, he was the man from the blonde student's apartment!

Magnificent Body was a player. Hadn't she seen him with two

women hanging off him? She heaved a sigh and set her half-finished tea on the small table beside the chair.

Of course he was a player, Pandora. Look at him, she thought in disgust. Even married women with many children and their grandmothers probably threw themselves at him.

It was a good thing she'd taken off when she had or else she could be sitting in his kitchen right now, about to become his next conquest.

The thought sent heat straight to her belly and lower.

Pandora picked up one of the carving chisels that she kept on the table and a chunk of rosewood that was slated to become the next worry box.

Would that be so bad? she wondered as she dug at the wood with a little more effort than necessary. Would falling into the player's bed honestly be so bad? At least she wouldn't die a dried up old virgin.

She imagined those strong hands on her naked skin, the weight of his firm body on top of her, the feel of his body hair moving against her smooth skin.

Stop it! She took another stab at the wood and caught her finger. Blood welled out of the cut.

"Dammit. Nothing has gone right all night. What's wrong with me?"

She tossed down the wood and chisel in disgust and went to the sink to clean the wound and bandage it. Instead of returning to her task she turned off all the lights, wrapped herself in her soft, old quilt, and laid on the worn leather couch that served as her bed.

Squirt jumped on top of her and settled on her hip, kneading her with his sharp little claws and rattling his contentment. Pandora reached a hand out from the quilt and plucked him off her hip. She cuddled him to her chest, enjoying his soft warmth, and let her thoughts drift.

Tomorrow night she would track down Luke and have a word with him, she decided. Warn him off the gang and thieving.

And she would be very sure to keep an eye out for Magnificent Body. It wouldn't do to run into him again. He was too . . . distracting. She needed to remain focused.

And on that thought, Pandora drifted off to sleep and dreamt of a man with smoky gray eyes and the body of a god.

CHAPTER 11

PANDORA WOKE AT DUSK. She normally got up shortly after noon and then took a quick nap before she left for work. She didn't like sleeping the daylight hours away and only being active at night. It felt too much like vampirism, and her life felt strange enough without adding *that* into the mix.

But apparently she'd needed to recharge her batteries because today she'd slept straight through to nightfall. She stretched and rolled onto her back, warm and relaxed, and waited for the lingering wisps of dreamworld to clear from her brain.

Squirt scrambled up onto her chest and mewed, bumping his head against her chin.

"All right, all right. I guess you're telling me you're hungry. How does such a little body manage to eat so much, I wonder?" Pandora yawned and threw the quilt aside, got to her feet with Squirt held in the palm of one hand. Although he had grown some he was still unbelievably tiny.

As she hadn't eaten since the previous day her own stomach was rumbling. She took the time to make and eat a full meal of ham steak, scrambled eggs, and home fries. She shared a spoonful of the eggs with the kitten but decided the ham was too salty for him. He tried to convince her otherwise, scrambling up her leg with his sharp claws pricking through her jeans.

"Ouch. No. This isn't good for you. Show some self-respect. Aren't cats supposed to act aloof and dignified?" Pandora plucked Squirt from her leg and set him on the floor next to his full food dish.

He ran straight back to her chair and mewed up at the table far over his head, turning in circles. Pandora sat to finish her meal. She bumped Squirt with her stockinged toe and rolled him over. He leaped up on stiff legs, fury written all over his tiny body, and leaped on her foot, clawing and biting her thick sock.

Laughter bubbled up in Pandora's chest. She was still grinning as she turned on the night light and slipped out the mudroom door to collect the night's worries.

A gentle south wind brought the smell of spring, the sounds of flocks of returning geese, and summer-like temperatures to the night air.

Pandora walked up to the marsh and listened to the familiar sounds of a warm spring night. The occasional duck chortled in the cattails, safely hidden for the night while it rested before tomorrow's flight. Tiny spring peepers provided background music with their throaty frog song.

The scent of marsh mud newly released from the ice hung on the air. Pandora felt contentment wash over her at the beautiful night. It was moments like these that reenergized her and enabled her to scour the city for the worst of people's worries.

She turned and continued north and west, crossed the bridge to French Island and headed to the southern tip. These weren't her usual hunting grounds but something had drawn her here tonight.

Experience had taught her to go out without a plan and let her feet take her where they wanted. Somehow it worked. Some might call it lazy or sloppy to work without a plan. She preferred to think of it as allowing her intuition to guide her.

Pandora cruised an affluent island neighborhood built next to the Mississippi River. Here stone walls divided well-kept lawns from flood waters, and docks, powerboats, and house boats extended the high-dollar properties into the river.

She listened to the squawk of a large raft of geese resting just offshore, and wondered what had disturbed them. A great-horned owl's quiet "hoo-hoo" sounded from a grove of large old maple trees on her left.

She hurried between two dark houses, her attention drawn to the last house in the cul-de-sac. The big river flowed behind the house and around the jutting peninsula where it was lit by the setting moon. The air here smelled richly of wet, earthy things and fresh green erupting after the long sleep of winter.

It was a neighborhood of privilege and quiet money. Of security and the residents' confidence of their place in the order of things.

Only the target house showed signs of anxiety. Large and modern in design with wide spans of glass looking out at the river and well-manicured grounds, it was another home that housed the well-to-do, the successful.

While some people believed that the possession of money wiped out all worries, Pandora knew better. Sure, it eliminated a lot—like where to find the money for rent and food—but worry, real worry, hit all strata of society.

She turned and moved smoothly down the side of the house, gliding along a stream of daffodils and newly emerged bedding plants toward the patch of light blazing from a first floor window.

The family's dog, an aged golden retriever, scented her and

stood at attention, then relaxed. Dogs liked her, even the ones trained to attack and maim. They were adept at telling friend from foe.

As she drew closer to the patch of light the strength of the worry grew. Pandora stood on the edge of darkness and tuned her senses.

Inside the house a man not far past middle-age, gray silvering his dark hair at the temples, paced in a room filled with floor to ceiling bookshelves and large, leather club chairs. A comfortable room she sensed, a man-cave for a man who enjoyed reading.

She felt a father's love and worry. Worry for his son, deployed to fight a war he didn't understand in a foreign country he didn't know. There was pride mixed with the worry, but the worry kept the man from sleeping.

He hadn't heard from his son in a few days and knew the fighting was heavy where the son's unit was located. The fear that he would soon receive notice of his son's death pressed on his chest and made it hard to breathe. Impossible to eat or sleep.

Pandora lifted her hand and began to grasp the threads of the man's worry and draw them out. She pulled and twirled them around her long, sensitive fingers, then rolled them off and compressed them into a small ball that she secured in a pocket.

She couldn't take it all, but she took enough to allow the man to rest and function.

She made her way out of the neighborhood and back across the bridge and headed south into downtown La Crosse. She walked quickly by the dark retail shops, bars, and restaurants, and skirted the parking garages where trouble often lurked.

The traffic lights flashed constant red or yellow. A car passed by blaring rock and roll. Someone tossed a large paper cup out of the rear window. Soda splashed on the sidewalk.

"Morons." Pandora bent to pick up the cup and placed it in a nearby trashcan. She hated litter and often stopped to pick it up while out at night. It never ceased to amaze her how poorly people treated their home.

Did they think that once the earth became uninhabitable they could just up and move? Like leaving one apartment for another? She shook off the pissy thoughts and picked up her pace. It was time to track down Luke and have a word with the boy.

She stopped by Luke's home first, hoping that he had come to his senses and was tucked into his bed with his siblings. The mother sat in the living room, slumped on a short couch watching television. Waiting for her son to come home.

Pandora scooted around the house and checked the kid's bedroom just to make sure, saw the empty bunk. So Luke was out again. With the gang member from last night or did he have a new partner?

She leaned against the house to think. The thieves wouldn't go back to the neighborhood where they'd been caught. Once caught, the cops would be keeping an eye out for them there.

Pandora left the house and headed north, watching the streets and shadows for any sign of the thieves. She had covered six blocks when she heard the distinctive hum of bicycle tires rolling fast over tar.

Somehow she knew it was Magnificent Body. The man who's house Luke had tried to rob was cruising this neighborhood. She'd know the sound of his tires anywhere. She stepped into the dark recess created by a porch and the front wall of a house and pulled her hood down low.

The bicyclist passed by and turned down the next street. Pandora waited without moving for several minutes to be sure he hadn't doubled back then hurried after him, her blood racing.

Finding Luke had become a priority mission for her. But she also needed to stay away from the man who was a player. A player who traveled the streets as she did.

Why did he do that? she wondered. What was he looking for?

CHAPTER 12

IT WAS a perfect night for cycling. The soft spring air flowed over Zee's bare arms and legs and blew his hair back from his face, carried the promise of the end of winter.

The physical activity made him feel alive and maybe a little more at peace with being stuck in La Crosse.

He still hadn't been able to speak with his father. It had occurred to him today after another failed attempt at contact that his father was avoiding him. But why? The situation made zero sense to Zee.

His father had contacted him in southern California and ordered him to La Crosse, Wisconsin. An important errand that only Zee could handle. Ordered him to stay here and await further instructions. And even though the situation made no sense to him, that's exactly what Zee would do.

Zee and his two brothers knew that once given an order they had to obey. Each of them had challenged that truth as young lads and learned the hard way that when Father told them to do something, they'd better do it or suffer the consequences.

He'd tried asking Pauli and Percy if they'd heard any rumors about why he was here but they had denied any knowledge.

Whether they lied or not he had no way of knowing. All three brothers could be consummate liars if it suited them.

His mother was no help either. When questioned directly she simply replied, "You'll have to talk to your father, Zee. This is none of my business. Try to be patient. He knows you're there. He'll get back to you I'm sure, all in good time."

Zee was nothing if not pragmatic. He would make the best of being stuck in middle America. He knew how to entertain himself. He spent time at the library devouring their book collections. He shopped for food daily and practiced cooking.

He joined a hot yoga class—where every female had asked him out, and now, much to his relief, ignored him after his steady refusals.

During the day he rode his Harley and explored outside of the city and at night he rode his bicycle and explored the city itself looking for the woman thief.

Zee knew that it was foolish to become obsessed over her but he still felt the sting of being duped, and he knew that wouldn't go away until he tracked her down and told her just what he thought about her. Maybe even had her arrested.

And so here he was, riding up and down streets and alleys looking for a dark cape because he had no idea what the woman looked like without it.

What color was her hair? Her eyes? Did she have freckles? Pock-marked or scarred skin? Was she old? Young? The frustration of not knowing made his legs work until he fairly flew through the neighborhoods, tires humming, leaning into the corners as if he was riding his motorcycle.

And then he thought he caught the barest glimmer of a cape disappearing around a corner.

"Dammit." Zee shot across the street and down a narrow dirt alley lined with small one-car garages and garbage bins. He shot out the opposite and looked to his left.

There! Just a glimpse, but he swore it was her. He banked hard left, nearly dumping the bike, and righted himself just before he plowed into a parked car. The near miss only served to infuriate him more.

He raced to the next corner, fully expecting to see the woman hurrying down the sidewalk, but the sidewalk was empty.

Where'd she go? There was no way she could walk, or even run, faster than he biked. She had to be here somewhere.

Of course, he realized. She's casing out houses here. There's no other explanation. A woman doesn't just vanish into the night.

He jumped the bike up over the curb and peddled slowly down the sidewalk, peering carefully between houses. He knew the thieves preferred a partially opened window and that's what she'd be searching for.

Where was her partner? There should be two of them out working the neighborhood. He stopped beneath a large ash tree and scoped out the houses. A middle-class, working neighborhood much like the one he currently lived in, he noted.

They were mostly two story homes, a mix of older brick and newer wood framed houses, well maintained, with front porches and small, grassy front yards. Late model or slightly older cars were parked in the driveways and at the curb in front of the homes.

Children's toys and small bikes decorated the yards of several houses. How could these thieves justify stealing from children? he wondered with disgust. They deserved to be tossed in jail.

He stood and waited. Motionless and patient like a hunter. Sooner or later one of the pair of thieves would show up, he felt sure of it.

His patience was rewarded twenty minutes later when he saw a boy of ten or eleven pop out from between two houses. A tall, lanky shadow detached itself from its hiding place next to a nearby front porch and met the boy.

Where was the woman? Zee knew he had seen her in the vicinity. He was about to blow his hiding place when he saw a flowing cape come running out of an alley halfway down the block. Satisfaction poured through him.

"Gotcha now," he whispered.

Zee rode up fast and braked to a stop next to the woman. The two boys took off running in opposite directions as he grabbed a fistful of cape in his left hand.

"We meet again, sweetheart. Maybe this time I'll get your name before you run off. Or before I drag you down to the police station, that is."

The woman whirled on him, furious. "You've ruined everything, you moron! Do you know how long I've been looking for that boy? Let go of me! What's wrong with you?"

"I'll tell you what's wrong with me, Miss Whoever You are. I don't like being played for a sucker. You got away last night before I realized you're one of them. You're a thief. Well played, darling, but you won't pull that off again, I promise you. I've got your number now."

He yanked the hood from the woman's head and caught his breath. She had to be the most beautiful woman he'd ever seen, next to his mother.

Thick, dark hair flowed to her shoulders and disappeared inside the cape. Large deep blue eyes—angry eyes that a man could get lost in—sparked at him from a classically sculpted face. Her full lips were puckered in an angry pout.

She shoved at him and broke the spell. "Get your hand off me, you moron. I haven't duped you. Idiot."

By Zeus, she was really steaming, Zee thought in admiration. He'd like to see all that passion channeled into another area—like the bedroom for instance. He bet she'd be amazing in bed. All that energy beneath him, wrapped around him . . .

It struck him then. He felt attracted to this caped thief,

attracted in a way he hadn't felt in months for a woman. No, he corrected, he felt attracted to her in a way he had never been attracted to a woman before. Like his blood simmered in his body and only needed her touch to put it at a full boil.

The realization pissed him off. He'd be damned before he let himself fall for a common thief.

"I want your name." His large hand bunched the cape tighter. "And then I'm calling the cops. You've robbed your last house, sister."

Somehow, despite being a good six inches shorter than Zee, the woman managed to throw him a haughty look down her perfect nose.

"You really are an idiot," she said. "Shows what you know. I am certainly not a thief."

"Then why have I found you hanging out with boys who *are* thieves two night running? Explain that, would you please? You can't, can you?"

"I'm out here, *moron*, because I'm trying to catch the younger boy you saw and talk him out of thieving. Not that it's any of your business. And who the hell are *you*, anyway?"

"I'm called Zee," he answered, almost absent-mindedly. He narrowed his eyes at her, trying to see inside her head. Was it possible she could be telling the truth? Or was she trying to scam him?

Pandora wished that Zee—what kind of name was that?— would let go of her cape. He was standing too close to her and it was muddling her brain. He was too big, too strong, too incredibly perfect and she didn't know how to handle that.

Not knowing how to handle it made her feel nervous and out of control. She didn't like feeling out of control. What if she did something crazy? Like throw herself into his incredibly masculine arms. She almost groaned aloud at the thought but caught herself.

Pull yourself together, Pandora. Focus. "May I go now?" she said aloud in her haughtiest tone. "Now that you've ruined everything?"

"I'm not sure." Zee felt reluctant to release the woman's cape. He would much rather pull her closer, much, much closer. In fact, he realized, he wanted to kiss her. So he did.

He gathered the front of her cape in his right hand and pulled her close, then tipped her chin up with his left hand and laid his lips on hers. A great shock ripped through his body and made his legs tremble.

Blast me, he thought. When has a kiss ever felt like that?

The shock of feeling a man's lips on hers stole the breath from Pandora's body. She felt like a live wire, nerves sizzling and snapping with pleasure. Without realizing what she did, she wrapped her arms around Zee's neck, pressing closer to him so she could feel his hard muscles through her cape.

And promptly heard a protesting cry from her pocket. She dropped her arms and stepped back.

Zee let go of her cape. "What the devil was that?"

Pandora reached into her cape and pulled out a tiny, angry kitten. She pulled him against her chest and stroked him.

Zee felt an insane rush of jealousy watching that lovely hand slide over the kitten's fur. He wanted those hands on his body, stroking him. Preferably while he was naked.

"This is Squirt," she answered, breaking into his hot fantasy. Her voice sounded like warm molasses.

"I guess he didn't like being squished," she added.

"You carry a kitten in your cape?" What kind of nut job carried a kitten around with her while she stole? He was about to ask her when he saw a police car turn the corner and head down the street towards them. He watched the car approach, then turned back to the woman.

The woman no longer stood beside him. She was like smoke.

Here one moment, gone the next. He twisted around, expecting to see her loping down the street but there was no sign of her anywhere.

How did she do that? he wondered. She was so smooth, he had to admire that in her. Once again she had played him and he'd fallen for it. And *that* pissed him off again. Royally pissed him off.

No woman had ever gotten the best of Zee. This one had done it not once, but twice now. Well, she couldn't hide from him forever. He'd find her again and next time he'd keep a tight hold on her.

Blast it. She'd disappeared again before he'd gotten her name, he realized in disgust. This place must be starting to rot his brain. He needed to finish his errand and get the hell out of here before he turned into a full moron.

Maybe the caped beauty had been right—maybe it was too late for Zee. Maybe he already *was* a moron.

On that pleasant thought he turned and greeted the police officers. Fortunately they were the two he had met the previous night. They left him alone with a warning not to try to do their jobs after Zee explained he'd been out looking for the thieves.

He gave up the search for the night. There was always tomorrow.

CHAPTER 13

PANDORA SLID through the dark shadows between two houses and put as much distance between her and the man on the bicycle as quickly as she could.

Luke would have to wait for another night. She needed to get home and regroup. Her lips still burned from when the man—Zee, that was his name—when Zee had kissed her.

She hoped the burn lasted a long, long time. It had to be the most exciting sensation she had ever experienced.

She had kept to the darker yards, checking the streets and alleys carefully for any sign of Zee before she hurried across, until she made it to her back hedge and through into her own yard.

What a relief to be home and safe. Safe from what, she didn't want to think about. She boxed the night's worries and set Squirt down. He immediately ran straight into the kitchen and waited for her to feed him.

Pandora brewed a cup of tea while Squirt ate. She was about to take her tea and sit by the fire when a knock sounded on the back door. Tea sloshed over the rim of the mug onto her hand and the floor.

Her heart raced. Had Zee somehow followed her? Tracked her here? The concept made her feel nervous and excited at the same time.

She needed to get a grip. There was no way Zee had followed her home. There could only be one person at the door, especially at this hour.

Pandora set the mug on the counter and walked through the mudroom to open the back door. As expected, Mrs. Mackleworth stood on the other side.

"Hello, dear. I haven't seen you in a couple of days and thought I'd just pop over to see how you're doing. You wouldn't have another cup of that tea, would you?"

She bustled past Pandora without waiting for an invite and removed her cloak, hung it on a hook and headed for the kitchen without waiting for an answer.

"Come in, Mrs. Mackleworth," Pandora said under her breath. "Make yourself at home." She closed the door and headed resignedly for the kitchen. She liked her neighbor, but she really wanted to be alone tonight so she could think about her encounter with Zee.

Mrs. Mackleworth had already found herself a mug and used the still hot water to pour herself a cup of tea. She took it to the chairs by the fireplace and settled her bulk into one.

"Come on, dear. Tell old Mackey what you've been up to." She pointed to the other chair. "Sit. Talk to me. I'm a lonely old woman and I need entertainment."

Oh, what the hell, Pandora thought. Why not? She scooped up Squirt as he wound through her legs and settled into the empty chair.

"You said that you know who I am, and what I do, right? You also said you knew my mother and my grandmother."

Mackey fluttered a hand. "Of course. You're one of the line of

Pandoras and you've dedicated your life to trying to collect other people's worries."

Pandora blinked. "Well, yeah. In a nutshell. Okay, so there's this one house that keeps drawing me back. A single mother and her five children live there. The place is tiny. I don't know how they do it. Anyway, the woman is a really good mother. She tries hard, but things keep happening. Money, or rather the lack of, is always a problem."

She stopped to sip her tea and stroke Squirt who lay stretched out in her lap.

"Her oldest child, a boy of ten or eleven, has fallen in with one of the gangs of thieves that work the city. I decided that maybe I could help the woman more by finding her son and talking with him, get him to quit the gang."

"That sounds like an admirable idea. How did it go?" Mackey asked.

"Not exactly as I planned. The first time I found the son, his name is Luke by the way—anyway, the first time I found Luke he was inside a man's house and the man came home. Long story short, I've seen the man before, in a neighbor's apartment, with two women hanging off him. He's a player."

The memory of Zee with the two women disturbed her so she shut it off.

"A player. He sounds interesting." Mackey leaned toward Pandora, her eyes sparkling with curiosity and humor. "Is he good-looking?"

"Good-looking? The man could be the poster boy for a statue of a Greek god. He's . . . words fail me."

Mackey sat back with a small smile. "Mmmmm, that handsome, huh?" Tell me more. There *is* more, isn't there?"

She wore a peacock blue pantsuit tonight, with a peach camisole and her usual layers of jewelry. Pandora was amused to see that like every other time she'd seen Mackey, tonight's

Birkenstocks matched the pantsuit. How many pairs of Birks did the woman own? she wondered, not for the first time.

Pandora thought about the *more* that had happened tonight and felt the heat rise to her face. She looked away from Mackey and down at Squirt who was purring loudly.

"Well, I-I saw him again tonight when I was out looking for Luke. We had a few words . . . " Did she really call him a moron? Twice? Pandora shook her head at herself. She had tried to shove him away. Might as well have shoved at a brick wall.

She recalled the feel of his strong hand gripping her cape, pulling her against that magnificent body, the way his full mouth had possessed hers. Without thinking, she touched her fingers lightly to her lips.

"What is it, dear?" Mackey had a full smile on her face. "Don't be embarrassed. I've had more crazy relationships with men than I can even recall. Nothing you can say will shock me. Tell me."

Pandora dropped her hand to lap. "Oh, it's nothing. We just had a few words and then . . . and then he kissed me." The heat flared in Pandora's cheeks and she knew they had turned a deep red.

"Kissed you! Ho-ho!" Mackey hooted a loud laugh that woke Squirt. He glared at her through slitted eyes, then went back to sleep.

"Was it a good kiss? You know, better than a quick peck?"

Pandora thought of the way her body had sizzled and her blood had fired when Zee's lips touched hers.

"I'd have to say that it was an amazing kiss," she admitted. "But it would be, wouldn't it? I mean, the guy's a player. He'd know how to kiss. Unlike me, who doesn't have a clue."

Mackey reached over and patted Pandora's arm. "Amazing is good, dear. I wouldn't concern myself about the rest of it. You could use a little romance in your life, Pandora. You're too lonely here, living in this big old house by yourself. It isn't a good life."

Pandora stiffened. "It's my life, Mackey," she said quietly. "I can't afford to let some playboy muck it up. Yes, I enjoyed the kiss, but what girl wouldn't. That's the end of it. I can't lose sight of the responsibility handed down to me."

Mackey shrugged one shoulder. "All right, dear. We'll talk about something else. Did I tell you I won big at Bingo this week?"

Forty-five minutes later, Pandora closed the mudroom door behind Mackey and leaned against it. She felt depressed, and so damn tired of being alone. Was Mackey right? Did she need some romance in her life?

She brushed her fingers gently over her lips and thought about Zee's kiss.

It was too bad there couldn't be more, she thought bitterly. If one kiss could make her feel the way his did, what would making love with him be like?

Earth shattering. Axis shifting. She knew that if she went to bed with Zee she would never be the same.

And that was the problem with players, wasn't it? She would change, but he wouldn't. There could be no future with Mr. Zee so she might as well put him from her mind.

She dressed for bed and brushed her teeth, wrapped inside her quilt and lay down to watch the dying fire. And imagined the feel of Zee's lips on hers. No matter how she tried to twist away from her reaction to his kiss the truth could not be denied.

She wanted more.

Finally she drifted off to sleep and dreamt of a handsome Greek god with dreamy gray eyes and the skills to light her on fire.

CHAPTER 14

THREE NIGHTS HAD PASSED and Zee hadn't run into the thieving woman again even though he spent hours biking every street and alley searching for her.

Frustrated thoughts of her and questions he desperately wanted answers to filled his every waking moment. Memories of the feel of her mouth beneath his filled his dreams when he slept. He woke feverish and wanting.

She haunted him and he hated her for it. No woman had ever affected him so deeply, especially one he'd known less than ten minutes total. Her effect on him bordered on the ridiculous.

He became obsessed with finding her, with learning her name, and with having her arrested. Once she was arrested he would have his answers and she would be out of his life. He could wash his hands of her and move on.

He could concentrate on his father's errand. According to his mother his father was due to return home from an unexpected trip early the next week—surely Father would explain the errand then.

In the meantime he spent every spare minute searching for

the mystery woman. Whenever he came across a pair of working thieves he stopped and watched them until he was sure she wasn't with them, then he called it in to Officer Stanhope, the older cop he had met the very first time he had seen Cape Woman.

Officer Stanhope joked that Zee was single-handedly cleaning up the community of thieves from the city and soon he'd be out of a job.

It was time to renew his search. Zee locked the kitchen door to his rented house, pulled his bicycle from the small detached garage, and slipped his sneakers into the toe clips.

During the day a taste of summer had arrived on a strong south wind the way it will sometimes. Cooler air would follow, but tonight felt hot and sticky, the air thick with moisture and heavy with the perfume of fresh damp earth.

Zee pulled off his long-sleeved tee and tossed it on the grass strip that ran between the house and the garage. Beneath it he wore a snug tank. He preferred to ride bare-chested, but unlike southern California or the French or Italian beaches, La Crosse was conservative. People here tended to cover their bodies. So he wore a tank.

He pedaled slowly through neighborhoods he had searched too many times to count. He was tooling down Albion Street one block over from Winter, near the section filled with lovely old mansions, when he saw Eleanor sitting on her steps.

He hadn't seen her since he first came to town and had accepted her invitation to party with her and another couple. He waved and tried to ride by but she called to him, then came running down the steps in her short shorts and flipflops, breasts bouncing in a too tight halter top.

Apparently Eleanor hadn't received the memo about middle America dress code.

Zee sighed, made a wide turn and pedaled back to her. Rudeness was not part of his makeup. He and his brothers might be superior to the average human male, but their mother had taught them to be respectful and humble.

"Zee!" Eleanor looked very pleased to see him, her breasts heaving from the short run.

"Hi, Eleanor. How've you been?" He straddled his bike on the sidewalk and looked down at the little blonde staring up at him. She was young, certainly attractive, but she lacked Cape Woman's beauty and innate charisma.

Disgusted with himself for making the comparison, he smiled down at Eleanor, then realized immediately that the smile was a mistake.

She gripped his forearm and batted her heavily mascaraed eyelashes at him. "I'm so happy to see you again, Zee. You left in a hurry that night, you naughty boy. I had plans for you and me."

"Did you now." Zee couldn't work up any interest. That was nothing new. Months before the conversation with his father ordering him to La Crosse, women had ceased to tempt him. Except for Cape Woman, blast her.

"Sorry about that," he said. "I remembered something I had to do that couldn't wait."

"Well, you're just out riding around now. I watched you passing back and forth at the intersections up and down King. Want to come in for a while? My date cancelled on me and I'm at loose ends."

"Come on," she begged, tugging on Zee's arm when he hesitated. "I have some cold brew. You must be thirsty."

"I guess I could come in for a few minutes. Thanks." Damn his mother and her insistence on politeness. Zee slid a leg off his bicycle and hefted it easily to his shoulder. He carried it up the steps and set it in the front hallway next to Eleanor's door, trying to ignore the greedy look in her eyes when she stared at his shorts-clad thighs.

The apartment looked exactly the same as his last visit, with its worn furniture and colorful throws. Empty soda and beer cans littered the small end tables while piles of textbooks and papers covered the small eating table. Discarded clothing was strewn about the floor and furniture and Zee smelled the faint odor of leftover food and dirty laundry.

Apparently Eleanor hadn't bothered to pick up for her cancelled date. He found himself wondering how Cape Woman lived. Did she have a small apartment like this? Or did she make enough on thieving to afford a real house?

"Here you go." Eleanor popped the top on a can of beer with one long, red-painted fingernail and handed it to Zee. She plopped on the couch with her own beer in hand and patted the cushion beside her.

"Sit. Tell me what you've been up to. Other than working out that is. You have an amazing body, Zee." She batted her eyes again.

"Ah. . . thanks." Accepting Eleanor's invitation had been a bad idea, rude or not, he realized. She wanted sex. With him. And he didn't want sex with her.

Thief or no thief, he wanted Cape Woman, dammit.

Zee took one of the chairs from the table, set it out of reach of Eleanor's long fingernails and straddled it. He ignored her pout and took a small swig of the beer, tried not to grimace. Coors. Like drinking horse piss. Plain water would have been a better choice. He cast about for something to say.

"So, Eleanor. Have you lived here long?"

Eleanor lifted her beer and drank half of it in one long swallow. He watched her throat work, knew she was striving for sexy, but all he could see was that a few years of drinking like that and she'd be puffy and fat.

"Yeah, I've been in this apartment a couple years now. I graduate at the end of this year. Why don't you sit next to me, Zee? There's plenty of room." She patted the cushion beside her again.

"Thanks, I'm okay. Do you know all of your neighbors? Or do you get a new batch with the new school year?" He took another small sip and tried not grimace.

Gad that stuff was bad. How long before he could leave without seeming rude?

Eleanor shrugged. Toyed with her halter so more of one breast showed. "I know some of them, I guess. Pretty much all of the apartments in the neighborhood change over with the school year, but the houses are mostly families who live and work in the city. Some of the big places over on Winter have been in the same families for generations. Why? You looking for someone in particular?"

"No. Well, maybe. But I doubt that you'd know her."

"Her? You looking for a woman, Zee?" Eleanor set her beer down on the floor and stood. She walked slowly over to Zee, swinging her hips in an exaggerated motion and running her tongue over her lips. She bent down when she reached him and swung her breasts close to his face.

"I'm a woman, Zee. And I'm right here." She placed a hand on either side of his head and tilted it up, set her lips to his.

Zee waited a few seconds, but he felt nothing. A big fat nothing. No blood boiling, no bolts of lightening zinging through him. He set the beer down and gripped Eleanor's wrists in his hands, pulled his head away from her.

"I appreciate the offer, Eleanor, really I do. You're an attractive woman, but I can't. I'm spoken for and I don't cheat."

As soon as he said the words Zee knew they were true. That damned Cape Woman had put her mark on him and spoiled him for anyone else.

Eleanor flounced back to the couch, picked up her beer and

chugged it. "Can't blame a girl for trying. You can see yourself out, cantcha?"

"Sure. Thanks for the beer. And—sorry." There really was nothing more to say. Zee let himself out of the apartment, grabbed his bike, and left the building. He stood for several minutes on the sidewalk, unsure what to do next.

The idea that Cape Woman was important to him shook him up. He never should have kissed her. Why had he kissed her? So she was beautiful—he'd kissed lots of beautiful women in his life. He enjoyed beautiful women.

But none of them had affected him the way she did.

He mounted the bike and began to pedal slowly, still feeling a little off his game. He wished Pauli hadn't left. He could talk to his youngest brother about this. Maybe Pauli had experience with kisses that set a man's blood to simmer and obsession.

Because that's what he was feeling, he realized. Obsession. Full blown obsession. He had become obsessed with a woman he didn't know. Blast it, he didn't even know her name or where she lived. But she had filled his thoughts since the first night he'd seen her outside his house.

Without taking a conscious direction, he crossed Winter Street and headed south. Fortunately the hour had grown late and the traffic almost non-existent so Zee could ride and think without putting himself or anyone else in danger.

He thought back to his last meeting with the woman, looking for clues to her identity. What had she said to him?

She had called him an idiot and a moron and shoved him. She had told him that she had been searching for a boy. Zee's brow furrowed as he leaned into another corner. Had she been telling the truth? Was it possible that she was *not* a thief?

But if Cape Woman was not a thief, what the hell was she doing roaming the city late at night? He needed to find her again.

He needed to get the truth from her and he needed to kiss her again.

Yeah, he needed to kiss her again to see if the last kiss had been an aberration.

Focused again, Zee picked up speed and began his systematic search for Cape Woman.

CHAPTER 15

PANDORA HEADED out for her nightly rounds a little earlier than usual. Despite constant searching she had had no luck locating Luke the last three nights. The last time she had seen him had been the night Zee scared him and his partner off.

Moron.

She slipped through the hedge and made her way between the student apartment buildings. She hadn't meant to peek into the blonde's window, but it had become such a habit she did it without thought.

What she saw made her feel as if someone had planted a small boulder of ice in her stomach.

Zee straddled a wooden chair, his back to the window. Still, Pandora knew it was him, knew that upper body clad in a snug sleeveless tee that showed off his impressive shoulders and biceps. Knew the thick black hair tied back in a short tail.

A stab of pain caught her breath in her chest and held it there as she watched the busty blonde student lean down and kiss Zee in a very thorough manner.

She knew how incredible those male lips felt. She fought down the jealousy that threatened to overwhelm her.

Player, she reminded herself as she hurried away. The man was a player. She shouldn't be surprised to see him kissing another woman. Just forget it. Forget about him. He meant nothing to her.

Easy to say. Impossible to do, she found, much to her disgust. Zee had filled her thoughts and dreams since the kiss he had planted on her several nights ago. And it was sad to admit, but she had been hoping to run into him again.

Enough of that, she scolded herself. Fantasies of Zee were nothing more than foolish dreams. Seeing Zee with the blonde tonight was a good thing. She needed to put him out of her mind completely and focus on her work and finding Luke.

That little kiss between him and the blonde was a good reminder that Zee was a player. PLAYER. Out of her league. Far beyond any of her experiences with men.

Still, seeing him kiss the blonde had hurt. She had concocted fantasies about the handsome Zee and it hurt to realize just how stupid and unrealistic they were.

Determined to put Zee out of her mind, Pandora turned south and headed down toward Luke's house. If the boy was home she would wait for him to come out.

Her plan had been to get out early and try to catch Luke before he hooked up with his gang, but when she arrived at the house and peered inside she could see she had missed him. She had no choice but to search for him again while she collected the night's worries.

Pandora pulled Squirt from his pocket and rubbed her face against his soft fur. He batted a paw at her cheek and made her laugh.

"At least I have you, my little friend," she whispered, and popped him back inside his pocket. She would take the kitten to one of the small parks that dotted the city and let him run around later, she decided. It was time they got back to their regular routine.

The night had turned hot and sultry, prompting those without air conditioners to open their windows. Canned laughter, explosions, and talking heads sounded from television sets turned up too loud. Music poured from some places, voices raised in anger came from others.

As the night wore on the noise quieted as people went to bed.

Pandora slipped through the now quiet neighborhoods in her wool cape, oblivious to the heat. Years of wearing wool through every season had conditioned her to its weight. The finely woven wool fibers breathed and kept her comfortable no matter the temperature.

She suspected there might have been a touch of magic involved in the making of the cape, but her mother had never come right out and admitted to it despite Pandora's pointed questions. It was simply another one of the many aspects of her strange life they had never gotten around to discussing.

Pandora heard the hum of bicycle tires and slipped behind a garage to wait for Zee to pass. Her heart leaped and she forced it down. Really, did he think she was so stupid that she wouldn't hear him coming?

She heard him turn down a nearby alley and ride off. If she hadn't seen Zee kissing the blonde she might have let him find her. But she had, so she wouldn't.

An hour later she came upon Luke and his new partner. Luke was about to enter a house while the older boy waited outside.

"Hold up there." Pandora left the shadows and stepped up to the older boy. "I'll give you ten seconds to get out of here before I call the cops. Ten. Nine . . ."

The boy glared at her, then much to Pandora's relief since she didn't have a phone, he turned and rabbited. She whirled around and grabbed Luke by the back of his shirt collar as he tried to follow.

"No you don't. You stand right there and you listen to me, young man. I've been trying to track you down for days. You do know that your mother waits up for you and worries, right?"

Luke shrugged, narrowed his eyes at Pandora. "What bizniss is it of yours, lady?"

"It's my *business*, Luke, because I care about your mother and your family. She carries a lot of weight on her shoulders. She works hard and does her best for you kids. Having her oldest child join a gang and become a thief is tearing her up."

Pandora felt the boy stiffen and tense and knew he was thinking about trying to run.

"Don't bother," she said, giving him a little shake. "I'm very fast and I'll only catch you again. Besides, I might be able to help." She had no idea why she'd said that, but it felt right. She decided to go with it.

"You take all the risks Luke, breaking into houses and stealing. I bet you don't see much of the profit from what you take. In fact, I'm willing to bet that your partner gets most of it. Right?"

Luke's eyes skittered away from hers. "So what? At least I bring in something. Ma can't do it all by herself."

Pandora looked down at the sullen and defiant young boy and her heart bled for him. In his own ignorant way he was trying to help care for his family.

"Where's your father? Doesn't he help out?"

Luke shrugged. "After Ma had Amy they got in a big fight and he left. Said he hadn't signed on to take care of all us kids. Ain't seen him since that night."

Pandora filed that piece of information away to deal with later. She was pretty sure the deadbeat dad should be on the hook for child support. She'd have to ask her neighbor if she knew anything about that. Mackey seemed to know about everything.

She looked down at Luke thoughtfully. "Seems to me what you're really after is a job, one that pays you an honest wage without a chance of going to jail."

"They won't put me in jail, I'm too young. That's why I do the inside work. Besides, who's going to hire a ten year old kid?" Luke tried to jerk free of Pandora's grip. "Let me go. I ain't done nothing to you."

"You haven't done anything," Pandora corrected automatically.

"Huh? That's what I said. You nuts, lady? What you doing out here anyhow?"

"I've been looking for *you*, knucklehead. You need a job, a respectable job that pays you honest wages. I have a job to offer you."

Luke's eyes went wide. "You do?" In the next instant his eyes narrowed and he pulled his head back. "Wait a minute, you ain't one of those weirdos who kidnap kids for sex slaves, are you?"

Pandora snatched her hand from Luke's collar. "Good lord, no! Oh my god, how would you even know about that? Euw! No, no, no."

She stared at the boy, horrified and sickened that someone so young would even know about the horrible things adults could do to children.

"No one's tried to. . ." she waved a hand in the air…"to you have they?"

"No! I'm not that desperate. Jeezus, lady."

"Okay, good. About that job." Squirt mewed and Pandora reached inside her cape for him and pulled him out. Luke's mouth dropped open.

"You carry a kitten in your cape?"

"Squirt hates being left alone. Want to hold him?" She held out the tiny ball of fluff and watched as Luke gently took him and held him to his chest. The tough-boy expression left his face and for the first time she saw the young, vulnerable boy underneath the tough facade.

"He's so tiny."

Pandora smiled. "Yeah, that's why I call him Squirt. So, I need someone to help me with yard work, and maybe some odd jobs around the house. I'll pay you cash and you keep it all, no sharing with anyone else except your mother. What do you think?"

Her yard could always use work, she reasoned. As for the odd jobs, it was hard to come up with any off the top of her head—after all, her house was stuffed to the rooftop with boxes—but she'd find something for the boy to do.

"What kind of yard work? Maybe I won't like it."

Still trying to be a tough guy, Pandora saw. She reached out and took Squirt back, put him in his pocket and pulled out the piece of paper with her address on it that she'd been carrying since she started looking for Luke.

"Does it matter? You'll like it better than being hauled down to a police station, I can promise you that. Besides, I think you'll like it just fine. Why don't you come by after school tomorrow? I'll have something for you so you can start right away."

She saw Luke's eyes widen in surprise when he looked at the address on the paper.

"I'll escort you home."

"You don't hafta do that. I know the way."

"Oh, I think I do. I wouldn't want some officer of the law to see you wandering the streets and assume you're up to no good. Let's go."

CHAPTER 16

ZEE STOOD in the shadow of a narrow two story brick house and watched Cape Woman with the boy. He'd seen her chase off the older boy and collar the young one. They appeared to be deep in conversation. He desperately wished he could hear what they were saying.

They had both seemed very tense at first, their body language stiff and defensive. But eventually they had relaxed some. He'd seen the kitten come out—why on earth did the woman carry a kitten around with her?—and then they headed down the block, the boy walking at Cape Woman's side.

What had that all been about? Zee wondered.

He knew better than to try to ride up on them—they would simply disappear on him. It had finally occurred to him, as he stood there in the quiet and listened to the soft murmur of their voices, that Cape Woman could hear his bicycle tires humming on the pavement.

No wonder she'd been able to avoid him, he thought with disgust. He didn't think about the noise while riding because he was so used to it, but standing here in the quiet, he realized he could hear sounds from several blocks away.

Moron. Cape Woman was right. He tucked the bicycle under a nearby porch and followed the pair on foot. They talked while they walked, and once Cape Woman laughed out loud, a soft, tinkling sound prettier than birdsong.

They stopped in front of a tiny wood-frame house with a dirt yard and slums on either side. Zee watched them shake hands. The woman stood and watched until the boy was safely inside, then turned and hurried off.

Zee stopped for a moment to peer inside the house, curious about its occupant. He saw a thin woman, her face lined with worry, confront the boy. The boy hugged the woman and spoke to her. Relief washed over the woman's face and she hugged the boy back.

Another mystery to add to the list of questions he had for Cape Woman when he caught up with her, Zee decided. He turned away from the house and hurried after the billowing cape.

The night air had become thicker and heavier. He knew that Cape Woman's cloak was wool, and heavy. He'd felt the finely woven fabric in his fist when he'd collared her last time. How did she stand to wear it in this heat? he wondered. The mysteries surrounding Cape Woman just kept piling up.

They passed the neighborhood where he'd stashed his bicycle. Zee hesitated for a brief moment, then decided to leave the bike where he'd hidden it rather than risk losing sight of the woman.

He wanted to see where she went next, what she did next. Most of all, he wanted to find out where she lived and her name. He would follow her all night if he had to, he decided. There was no way he was going to let her disappear on him again.

They headed to the center of La Crosse and turned up Albion Street. A little frisson of shock hit Zee when he saw the woman turn into the drive next to Eleanor's apartment.

No. She can't possibly live there. That would be too ironic. He stood in the deep shadow of the building next to Eleanor's and watched the woman cross the dirt parking lot filled with older economy cars—student cars. Then she disappeared in the shadow of a tall hedge.

What?

Zee hurried across the lot after her, angry at himself for not stopping her sooner. He came to the thick hedge and walked along it to the end, where it connected with a cross street. There was no sign of the woman.

Zee turned and hurried back, followed the hedge to the opposite edge where it ended in an alley.

"Blast it." Zee hurried back to the last place he had seen the woman and searched the hedge carefully. It took him several minutes to find the narrow opening.

"Ho-ho, I've got you now," he said quietly as he eased through the thick growth. Stiff branches clawed at him and scratched his arms, chest, and back, but Zee barely felt them. The thrill of finally pinning his quarry and getting some answers made his blood run hot.

He popped through the hedge and waited for his eyes to adjust to the darkness. He was in a large private yard the size of a small park, he realized.

Thick-trunked trees towered overhead. He could make out the outlines of flowerbeds along the back wall of the large house and also surrounding the two-story stone carriage house that filled the back corner of the yard to his right.

The house—more of a small castle, really—dominated the yard. A dim light shone through a back window. He saw a shadow block out the light, then pass by and stop at a wide wooden door.

Satisfaction swept through Zee. They would finish this tonight. She couldn't run away now. He crossed the yard quickly and silently, stopping several feet behind the woman, and waited to see what she would do.

As she bent to put the old iron key in the lock, a shiver passed down Pandora's neck and back. She jerked her head up and whirled around, cape swirling, then let out a strangled scream when she saw a man standing a few short feet behind her.

She staggered back until she was pressed up against the door.

"So, we meet again," Zee said, his voice low and growly. "Looks like I've arrived in time to save these people from being robbed by a common thief."

Pandora huffed out a sigh of relief when she saw that it was Zee. She fisted her hand around the key and shook it in his face.

"You followed me! You have no right to be here. Now get out before I call the police and report a strange man trespassing." She felt angry at the jolt of fear Zee had given her, but more disgusted with herself for the way her body quivered at the sight of him. Her female hormones were betraying her and she didn't care for it one little bit.

"If this is your house—and I truly doubt that—then the thieving business must be very, very lucrative. Aren't you going to invite me in?" Zee stepped forward and placed a hand against the wall beside the door and leaned in on her.

The flash of uncertainty in her eyes gave him a great deal of satisfaction. He was in charge here, and the quicker she understood that, the better. He chose to ignore the fact that standing so near to her clouded his mind.

Pandora angled her shoulder, trying to put her back to Zee while she collected her suddenly scattered brain. She fumbled and dropped the key, picked it up. When she tried to place it into the keyhole again she found Zee's large hand covering hers.

"Allow me." He took the key from her and examined it. Nearly four inches long, it was forged from heavy black iron and sported an ornate design on the end.

Zee inserted the key and opened the door but Cape Woman

didn't move. "As I suspected," he said quietly. "Not your house. Did you steal this key?"

Pandora grabbed the key from him and stepped quickly into the mudroom.

"It's my house and you are not invited in." She started to close the mudroom door but Zee stepped inside and blocked it with his body.

"You aren't getting rid of me that easily. I want to know who you are, lady, and I want to know why you roam this city at night, and I really want to know why you carry a kitten around with you," he added as Pandora pulled Squirt from an inside pocket and set him on the floor.

She stared at the cape. Almost seemed unsure what to do with it, he noticed. Maybe this wasn't her house after all. Finally she hung the cape on a wooden peg next to the door and turned to him with her hands on her hips.

He couldn't help but notice how long and lean her legs were, dressed in faded jeans that also showed off a tight, muscled ass. A snug, rose-colored tee stretched over breasts that were small and firm. His breath shortened and he jerked his eyes to her face, found her glaring at him.

"What do you want, Zee? Aren't there enough willing women in La Crosse for you? Why chase me? Why not go back to the blonde student's apartment? I saw you there earlier. She was definitely willing."

She hadn't meant to mention the blonde. Why had she mentioned the blonde? Zee made her nervous. Part of her wanted to boot him out the door, and part of her very much wanted him to stay. She hated the turmoil he created in her.

Instead of answering, Zee looked around the spacious mudroom.

The mudroom walls had been paneled in cedar now grayed

with age, and the floor tiled in blue slate. A painted tin ceiling, once white, now yellow with age, completed the room.

It spoke of class and old money. He wondered what the rest of the house looked like.

Suddenly he lost his appetite for intimidation and games.

"Who are you? At least tell me your name." The kitten came flouncing back into the mudroom, meowing madly. He reached down and picked it up, rubbed his thumb against its tiny little back.

"Pandora. My name is Pandora. What do you want, Zee? I'm tired and I need to come up with some legitimate chores by tomorrow afternoon to keep a young boy out of trouble."

"Let's talk. I just want to talk, Pandora." Her name felt right on his tongue. Pandora. She of beauty and legend.

"Do you have any beer?" he asked.

Pandora shook her head and reached out for Squirt. Tucking him to her chest she turned away and walked out of the mudroom.

"No. No beer or wine. I don't like to drink alone so I don't keep alcohol in the house. I have tea or water."

She wasn't going to insist that he leave. The relief that passed through Zee's body left him weak. "Tea. Tea's good. Can I help you make it?"

She turned her head and smirked at him. "Thank you, but I think I can handle it. I have to feed Squirt first, then I'll make the tea."

Zee followed her into the old-fashioned kitchen, wandering and lightly touching things while Pandora watched him from the corner of her eyes as she set about feeding Squirt and making the tea.

He noted the old, scarred cherry table and floor-to-ceiling walnut buffet, the well-worn leather chairs and couch, and the heavy, serviceable dishes.

He stirred the embers and added a log to the fire, noticed the carving tools and block of wood with it's half-finished design. He picked it up and ran a finger gently over the intricate pattern. The workmanship was superb, as fine as any museum-quality piece he'd ever seen.

"This is very good. Who carves?"

Pandora glanced his way, saw that Zee held her latest box. Her stomach clenched. Would he ask questions? If he asked she'd have to tell him. If she told him she'd never see him again.

"I carve." She tried to keep her tone casual, but when she saw the surprise on his face, she instantly felt defensive. "What?" she asked, fists on her hips. "You don't think a woman can carve? Or are you surprised because you don't believe that *I* could possibly be creative? Oh, that's right, you think I'm a thief. Well, you don't know spit, Zee."

She slammed a mug of tea on one of the small tables that sat beside the chairs and plunked herself down in the one with the carving tools.

Zee narrowed his eyes at her. She sure was a prickly thing. He sat in the other chair and stretched his legs out in front of him. He caught Pandora's gaze running up his thighs before she frowned and stared into the fire.

Good, he thought smugly. She wasn't as indifferent to him as he feared. Now to find a chink in that thick wall she carried around for protection. Zee sipped his tea and waited for her to settle.

"So, this must be one of the finest houses in La Crosse. Has it been in your family long?"

"Yes. My great-great, many-greats, grandfather built it." She stared into the fire when she spoke. She didn't dare look at Zee, afraid he would see the way her blood hummed at the sight of his incredible, and mostly naked body. God he was built. And surely the most handsome man she had ever seen.

"I'd love a tour of the house," Zee said. "I'm a big fan of architecture. I've studied it in every country I've lived in."

"No." A tour of the house? Out of the question. Besides the fact that a person could barely move through all the boxes stacked to the ceiling. . . there was no besides the fact. What on earth would Zee say when he saw all those boxes? What if he opened one? The sooner he left the better.

"You almost finished with your tea?" she asked. "I have things to do before I go to bed."

Zee took a small sip. "No." Obviously talking about the house was not the way to get Pandora to open up. He had thought that once he cornered her he'd get his answers. Instead he had more questions. The woman fascinated him. He needed to find a chink in her armor.

And then he knew what to ask.

"So, you mentioned finding chores for some boy. Tell me about that."

Squirt, supper finished, came racing over to Pandora's chair and pulled himself up her calf with his sharp claws. He settled into her lap and began to clean himself. Having the kitten with her calmed her nerves. She could see no harm in telling Zee about Luke. At least Luke was a safe subject.

"There's this kid, a young boy named Luke. He's only ten years old. His father deserted his mother and five children and they're struggling. She works hard at holding the family together, but it's hard, you know?"

She risked looking at Zee to see if he understood. She found those smokey gray eyes watching her and felt a little breathless. He nodded in answer. She forced herself to take a deep breath and went on.

"Luke got drafted by one of the gangs who steal. I . . . the first time we met I had tracked him to your house. I was waiting for him to come out so I could talk to him but you showed up on your bicycle. I was afraid you'd catch him inside, so I jumped on his partner, the older boy who always waits outside."

"You mean that's when you fell out of the tree." Zee's mouth thinned at the memory. "The cops arrested the older kid, but you disappeared. You have a habit of doing that."

Pandora waved a hand in the air. "Yes, well, anyway, the second time I found Luke you showed up again and grabbed me. He got away."

"Hmm. Luke got away and I kissed you, if I remember right." Oh, he remembered only too well, he thought. He shifted in the chair, aware of a sudden tightening in his groin at the memory of the heat in that kiss.

She refused to acknowledge that kiss. She did not want to think about it, especially with Zee sitting not three feet away from her.

"So, anyway . . . tonight I finally found Luke and had a chance to talk with him. He joined the gang to help his family, but at heart he's an honest kid. His mother is bringing him up right. He knows right from wrong, but feels that as he's now the man of the family, it's up to him to help in any way he can.

"Tonight I offered him an alternative to stealing. I hired him to do yard work and odd chores for me. He starts tomorrow after school so I really do need to come up with some easy chores, at least until we get a feel for each other and I can see how much he can handle."

She stole a quick look at Zee's face and saw the surprise in his eyes. That he would be surprised by her action irritated her. Just what kind of person did he think she was? Oh, that's right, she reminded herself. He thought she was a thief. She glared back at him, happy to be angry again.

"What? You don't believe me?"

"I believe you." Zee reached over and placed his hand over hers. "It's just not what I expected. To be honest I thought you were one of the thieves. In my defense it was the only explanation I could come up with for why you were out there at night." He saw Pandora stiffen.

"You're doing a good thing, Pandora," he hastened to add. "The kid's lucky to have someone like you who cares."

Zee stood and pulled her to her feet so they stood mere inches from each other. He lifted her hand and brushed his lips softly across the back of it, noting with pleasure the shiver that went through her body when he did.

He turned the hand over and ran his thumb over its calloused palm, so different from the silky smooth back, then released it.

"I think I should go. I'd like to come back and see you again. May I come tomorrow?"

Player, Pandora reminded herself. This man was a player. You saw him kissing blondie only a few short hours ago.

"Yes, tomorrow would be fine," she heard herself answer. She walked him to the door and closed it behind him, then leaned her forehead against it.

What was she thinking, telling Zee he could come back? The man would only bring her heartache.

ZEE WASN'T sure why he had cut his visit with Pandora short the previous night, but it had seemed like the right thing to do. He had sensed a vulnerability in her that made him not want to press too hard too fast.

On top of that his confidence had returned now that he knew her name and where she lived. The hunt was over. Now he had the pleasure of getting to know and seduce her.

He wheeled his bicycled into her drive and let out a low whistle when he saw the front of the house. Castle indeed, he thought. The place was magnificent with its round turrets and covered stone balconies and a slate roof that rose four stories and yet was dwarfed by the ancient trees growing around it.

He dismounted the bike and set it inside the covered entrance. The carved front door sported a series of small, diamond-shaped leaded glass windows. Original, he decided, noting the small bubbles trapped in the wavy glass.

He lifted the heavy iron knocker and let it drop with a flat thud. If Pandora was in the kitchen she would never hear it.

Frowning, Zee located a doorbell and pushed it, but heard nothing chime inside. He stepped out from under the portico and walked around the side of the house, checking the windows. Drapes had been closed over each one, all the way to the attic floor.

What did Pandora and her family have against daylight? Or had the house been closed up?

Anger began to spark in Zee's blood. If Pandora had changed her mind and thought he'd go away quietly, she had a hard lesson coming. The sons of Zeus did not give up.

He walked briskly down a narrow stone path along the side of the house, anxious to confront the aggravating Pandora. Daffodils and colorful tulips guarded the bottom of the house's pale stone walls. Purple and white croci transformed the lawn on his right to a colorful carpet.

He heard a woman shout in the back yard. Pandora!

Prepared to play the hero, Zee sprinted to the back corner of the house only to stop short. Pandora and a small brown-haired boy were washing an automobile that belonged in an auto buff's collection.

Fortunately she hadn't seem him act the fool. Zee slipped off his backpack and set it next to the house before sauntering over for a better look at the car. An old Thunderbird in baby blue with original paint and white and black leather interior, the car appeared to be in mint condition.

"That's quite a car you have there."

He took a perverse satisfaction when Pandora squealed and whirled around. He hadn't counted on the hose in her hand spraying across his shirt.

"Oops, sorry."

Zee looked down at his dripping tee shirt, then up at Pandora. Her blue eyes sparkled with laughter. She had pinned her long hair into some sort of bun on top of her head and wore ragged cut-off shorts and a cotton man's shirt knotted at the waist.

Even dressed in rags, with wisps of hair that had escaped plastered to her face and neck, she was easily the most beautiful woman he'd ever seen.

The young boy hooted with laughter and gave Zee a gap-toothed grin, pointing at Zee's wet tee. It was enough to break the spell.

Before he could say anything else and regain the upper hand, Pandora let go of the spray nozzle and tossed Zee a chamois cloth. "If you're going to stand around you might as well help. Right, Luke?"

"Right, Miss Pandora. Everyone has to pull their weight. That's what my Ma says."

"Well your mother is a very wise woman. When we finish I'll give you a ride home in the Thunderbird. Would you like that?"

"Really?" Luke's brown eyes were wide with excitement. "Can I come back tomorrow?"

Zee looked into Luke's worshipful face and realized that he wasn't Pandora's only conquest. Luke evidently thought the world of her and the boy had only met her the previous night.

"Of course you may come tomorrow," Pandora answered. "I have plenty of chores for you to help me with, Luke." She squatted down to look the boy square in the eyes. "You may come as often as you like. Now that we're friends, you'll always be welcome here wether you come to help me or just to visit."

They all set to work drying and waxing the car, then Pandora drove Luke home. Zee had to ride in the back seat but he didn't mind. Unlike newer cars, the T-bird's back seat was deep and roomy and extremely comfortable.

Besides, sitting behind Pandora gave him a chance to study her and listen to her finesse information out of Luke. He had to admire her technique—she was so smooth the boy didn't realize he was being interrogated.

Not only smooth, Zee realized. Pandora genuinely cared about Luke and what he had to say, and the boy sensed it and responded to it. Occasionally Zee caught her watching him in the rearview mirror and he smiled at her. Once he winked and was absurdly pleased to see her blush.

They dropped Luke off in front of his house with a promise to see him tomorrow and Zee climbed into the front seat for the trip back.

"It's a wonderful thing you're doing for that boy, Pandora," he said as he settled in. "You've changed his life and he'll never forget you for that."

Pandora shrugged and tried to act nonchalant but he saw the faint blush on her neck and cheeks and knew she was pleased by the compliment.

"I brought the fixings for dinner. Thought I'd cook for the both of us tonight."

Pandora's eyes cut over to him in surprise. "You cook?"

Zee pretended to scowl. "I'm not just a pretty face, you know. My mother insisted that her sons learn how to fend for ourselves. So yes I cook. And I'd like to cook for you tonight. You okay with that?"

Pandora smiled at him, a dimple appearing in her left cheek.

"No man has ever cooked for me before. Yes, you may cook dinner."

The meal went well in Zee's opinion. He had kept it simple: steak and salad with a fine bottle of Cabernet that, after much persuading, Pandora agreed to partake of a half-glass.

He couldn't help but notice how Pandora deflected his attempts to learn more about her and her family, so he kept the conversation light and entertained her with stories about the different places he had lived and some of the scrapes he and Pauli had gotten into in their younger days.

Pandora laughed in all the right places and seemed to enjoy herself, but when the meal was finished she told him he had to leave.

"I'll do the dishes," she said as she herded him to the mudroom. "You cooked. Thank you for a wonderful meal and the company, I really enjoyed myself."

Zee stopped in the middle of the mudroom. "Then why do I have to leave?" he asked. He didn't want to leave, dammit. He wanted to stay, drink more wine, maybe sneak in a kiss or two—or more.

"You have to leave because I have things to do." She gave him a gentle shove toward the door.

Zee took the opportunity to grab her hands and pull her to him. He wrapped his arms around her shoulders and held her tight, then eased back a bit and leaned his face down, brushing his lips against her hair.

"Are you sure you want me to leave?" he whispered. He felt Pandora tremble in his arms and relaxed, sure that she was going to change her mind.

But she surprised him. He felt her nod against his chest.

"Yes. You have to go."

Zee heaved a sigh and released her. "All right, I'll go. It's never been my way to force a woman if she doesn't want me."

He waited a beat, sure that Pandora would change her mind. She obviously wanted him—at least he felt pretty sure she did. Uncertainty was a new experience for him and he found he didn't like it one little bit.

When she said nothing he stepped away from her. Pandora looked at him then and he saw the regret in her eyes.

"Tomorrow? Same time and place?" he asked.

"You-you want to come back?"

"Hell yes. Tomorrow. I look forward to seeing what chore you come up with for all of us." The smile she gave him then was so brilliant it almost undid him. He thought maybe he'd do just about anything to see her smile like that again.

Zee kissed Pandora's cheek and let himself out. As he bicycled home to change for his night ride he wondered what he was getting himself into.

No woman had ever resisted him. Was that Pandora's attraction? Was it her kindness toward young Luke, her impossibly tiny kitten, or the mystery that surrounded her?

Whatever the attraction, he had no intention of stepping away until he knew the answer.

CHAPTER 18

AFTER ZEE LEFT, Pandora cleaned the kitchen and prepared for the night. Much to her surprise dinner with Zee had been relaxed and fun. She found that there was more to him than a great body and the face of a fallen angel. He was an interesting man, full of stories about places she'd dreamed of but had never seen.

And he'd been good with Luke. She gave him big points for that. He had engaged the boy while they worked on the car, listened to him, and treated him as an equal. For that fact alone, Zee had risen in her estimation.

He was still a Player, but now he was a Player with depth.

She found herself humming a favorite tune of her mother's while she dressed to go out. She would have preferred to stay in and relax by the fire. Stay in and think about Zee and Luke, but she had a job to do.

She was tired from all the activity earlier that day, but worries never stopped. And because they never stopped she had a job to do. She had never missed a night since the first night at her mother's side learning the ropes. She would not be the first Pandora to break the chain that extended thousands of years into the past.

Her feet led her towards Losey Boulevard and Zee's neighborhood. She hesitated briefly when she saw where she was going and wondered if her subconscious was looking for Zee, but decided that she trusted her instincts to take her where she was needed most.

She found herself standing in front of a very nice Craftsmen style home, a popular style in La Crosse from the Frank Lloyd Wright era. Built of wood and stucco, lit leaded windows throughout the house told her that the residents were awake. Awake and troubled.

She slid soundlessly down the side yard, stopping at each window until she found the family gathered in a large rear bedroom. A young mother lay dying on a queen-sized four poster bed with her husband and three children gathered around her.

It took several minutes of observation for Pandora to realize that she wasn't here to help the father. While his deep grief was obvious, this time her task was to relieve the woman of her worries so she could die in peace, knowing that her family loved each other and would be okay without her.

Pandora lifted her hand and began the intricate process of grasping and pulling the thick threads of worry from the woman's mind. She wound them round and round until they formed a tight ball and slipped it into an empty pocket.

She waited a moment to see if there was more for her to do. She watched the woman's body relax. The mother smiled and grasped her husband's and children's hands.

Mission accomplished. Though sad, everyone would get through the ordeal. Where resentment could have festered, instead they would remember their mother's love and bravery with love of their own and become better people for it.

Satisfied, Pandora slipped through the back yard and into a yard on the next block where she came face to face with Zee. He stood next to his bicycle, dressed in silky shorts and a snug tee that defined every muscle.

"What are you doing here?" she demanded. Fear made her angry. "Are you following me again?" Her heart thudded in her chest. How much had he seen?

"I live here, Pandora." Zee gestured toward the house beside them. "What are you doing here seems to be the better question, I think. Were you looking for me?"

He hoped that she was, hoped that she had changed her mind about wanting more from their evening together, but he was fairly sure she was out and up to her tricks, whatever those were.

"I-I had business in the neighborhood. I have to go." She hurried off, her cloak billowing behind her.

Zee made no attempt to stop her. He looked thoughtfully at the house that abutted the rear of his place. He knew the mother who lived there had lost her battle with cancer. Was Pandora taking advantage of the family's grief to rob them?

He was back to believing Pandora was a thief again, he thought with disgust. Just when he'd begun to believe she was a good person, and that angered him.

Blast it, he wanted answers. Who the devil was she and why did she roam the city all night dressed in that wool cloak?

Zee put his bike back in the garage and locked it, then headed after Pandora at a jog. He was determined to get answers, and while he hated to be sneaky about it, he saw no other way.

He caught up with her four blocks away, hurrying south, her dark cape flowing behind her. She passed by several men who seemed not to notice her and wasn't that strange?

She was far too beautiful to be ignored and most men out at this time of night would be up to no good. Thieves, druggies, rapists, partiers too wasted to find their way home—any of them would have at least tried to speak to her. Yet they all remained silent and acted as if she didn't exist. Curiouser and curiouser, mused Zee.

He watched her dart between two houses and silently crept up behind her. Not so close that she would sense him but close enough to watch her.

What he saw baffled him. She peered into windows as she worked her way around the small brick house, stopped beside a lit one, did a strangely beautiful dance with her hands, and tucked something inside her cape. Then hurried off.

Zee followed Pandora for several hours and watched the same ritual repeated over and over. Not only did nobody notice her on the street—even when she passed close by them—but she never entered any of the houses she chose. She merely performed her strange dance and left.

Only after he followed her back to her home and watched her let herself safely inside did he head back to his own house to mull over what he'd seen.

He suspected that the cloak held some sort of power to render Pandora invisible, or if not invisible, then to help her blend with the shadows.

The relief he felt, knowing that she was protected while she did whatever it was she did, surprised him. Caring about a woman was new territory for him.

Until recently the women in Zee's life were enjoyed and then forgotten. He treated them well. He always treated his dates well. But they meant little more than an evening's—or possibly a few day's—worth of entertainment before he moved on.

Now he found himself entangled with a mysterious woman who intrigued him. One who made him want . . . more. He realized that he felt protective toward Pandora, and the zing she put in his blood also made him feel possessive of her.

All foolish emotions since they barely knew one another.

Zee scowled. He really needed to get out of La Crosse. Five

more days before his father returned and he could complete his errand.

Then he was gone, whether he'd figured out the mystery of Pandora or not he promised himself. He needed to get back to his easy lifestyle.

One that did not include a mysterious woman who made him want.

When Zee arrived at Pandora's the next afternoon he found her and Luke pulling items from the carriage house. The drive and yard in front of the ornate two-story stone building held a wide assortment of furniture and mirrors, yard ornaments and sporting goods—many of them first class antiques in like new condition.

Luke wheeled a shiny black ten-speed out of the wide, open door and leaned it against the building. Other than two flat tires it looked as if it had just come off a bike shop floor.

"That was mine," Pandora told Luke, hurrying over to him. "There should be a tire pump in there too. I usually kept them together. Why don't you see if you can find it and we'll fill those flats."

Luke darted back inside and Pandora turned with a smile. Her smile faltered a little when she saw Zee standing there. He saw her take a deep breath, noticed the light bruising under her beautiful eyes that told him she hadn't slept well last night.

Well, tough, neither had he.

"You have some nice stuff here," he said, walking over to her. "Some of it would sell well at auction."

Pandora looked at the odd pieces spread around her and shrugged.

"Maybe. The Jones family has a tendency to hoard. I couldn't sell them, they're part of the family history."

Before Zee could question her, Luke came running out of the carriage house with the tire pump raised triumphantly in his hand.

"I found it! How does it work?"

"Here, let me." Zee took the pump from Luke and showed him how to attach it to the tire tube nozzle and then pump. He supervised Luke as the boy did the rear tire by himself, eyes shining.

"Looks like it's good to go," Pandora said. "Why don't you try her out, Luke? I'm sure Zee can adjust the seat to fit you."

"Really? I can ride it? I had a bike once but I outgrew it so Sadie has it now. Ma doesn't have the money to buy me a new one. I was collecting aluminum cans to save for one but Ma needed to buy medicine for the baby so gave what I saved to her. Now I have to start over."

Zee lowered the bicycle seat all the way. It was still a tad too high for Luke's short legs, but he didn't seem to mind. He took off down the drive whooping, and weaved his way on the lawn through the trees coming back.

"This is a great bike. You should ride it more, Miss Pandora," Luke said when he came back and stopped with a flourish, his face bright with happiness.

Pandora tousled Luke's hair and smiled at him. "I used to ride it all the time, but I have other interests now. May I gift it to you, Luke? It seems a shame to let such a fine bicycle sit unused."

Luke's face fell. He climbed off the bike and leaned it against the carriage house.

"Thank you, Miss Pandora, but I couldn't accept such an expensive gift. My Ma wouldn't like it."

Pandora nodded thoughtfully. "How about this then? I'll trade you the bike for your work today and over the next two days. Does that sound fair?"

"Take it Luke, it's a good offer. Fair to both parties." Zee put his hand on Luke's shoulder. "I rode my bike here. How about if we take a quick spin around the neighborhood so you can try out all the gears in case it needs any adjustments?"

He winked at Pandora. "We'll be back in a few."

Pandora watched the two males ride down the driveway and pressed her hand to her belly to stop the fluttering.

She had expected Zee to be angry with her after running into him last night, but he'd surprised her with his pleasantness. Was he too pleasant? she wondered. What was he up to? She wished she could read him better.

After Luke and Zee had returned and helped to neatly stack the stuff on one side of the carriage house, Zee offered to ride home with Luke. Before he left, he lifted Pandora's chin and brushed his lips lightly over hers.

"Your turn to cook dinner tonight. I'll see Luke home and come back." He left before she could answer.

She brushed her fingers over her lips. The man's touch made her brain turn to mush. Player. Player. She had to remember that Zee kissed women all the time. She had to resist.

Oh, but it was so hard to resist something that felt so incredibly wonderful. Would it really be so awful if she gave in and allowed herself to experience what making love would feel like with Zee? If not Zee, then who? It wasn't like she had suitors beating down her door.

Pandora hurried into the house to change and start dinner. She would play it by ear, she decided. If it felt right she would allow Zee to seduce her.

She went to work on dinner with a knot of anticipation in her belly.

CHAPTER 19

FORTUNATELY FOR ZEE LUKE chattered all the way to his house so Zee wasn't required to say much. Kissing Pandora, even just the light touch he had given her, had been a tactical error. Every time he touched her his desire for her grew.

So, he decided, he would not touch her again until she answered some of his questions. It wouldn't be easy keeping his hands off that lovely body, but he was the son of Zeus, wasn't he? He could do anything he set his mind to. Surely he could keep his hands to himself.

Back at Pandora's he rapped twice on the mudroom door and let himself in. Squirt came skittering out on the slate floor and tumbled at his feet. Chuckling, Zee reached down and plucked up the tiny kitten by the scruff of the neck and held him in front of his face.

"What are you up to, little guy? You protecting the lady of the house?" Big gray eyes looked back at him and the kitten let out a pitiful meow. Zee tucked him next to his chest and stroked until the kitten purred.

"That's better, huh? No worries about me, little guy. I mean your mistress no harm."

He walked into the kitchen and found Pandora up to her elbows in flour and butter. Something aromatic simmered on the stovetop and made his mouth water.

"There's wine left from last night. Could you pour me a half glass, please?" Pandora reached up to brush a loose hank of hair from her face and left a smudge of white flour behind.

Zee resisted the powerful urge to wipe the smudge away. She had exchanged her jeans and tee for blue cotton shorts and a white tank that showed off her long, toned arms and legs.

He wanted to start at her pretty bare toes and work his tongue from one end of her body to the other. He wanted—stop it, he chided himself. You're acting like a teenage boy with his first real crush. Focus. Pour wine.

"Are you all right?" Pandora looked at him, a line of worry formed between her elegant dark eyebrows. "I'm making chicken pot pie for dinner. It's one of my favorite comfort foods. I hope you like it."

"Sounds good." With studied nonchalance, Zee turned away, pulled two old wine glasses from the buffet and poured the wine. He handed her a glass and toasted her.

"That was nice of you, giving Luke that bike," he said. "I know I said this yesterday, but he's lucky to have you for a friend. How did you say you met him?" He studied her face closely while he waited for her answer, expecting her to lie.

Pandora concentrated on rolling out the pie crust. She was a good cook and enjoyed cooking. It was a treat to have somebody else to cook for. She only wished Zee could just be there and not want to dig into her life.

But he wasn't the type of person to take things at their surface or to let something go once he became interested in it. She knew that about him even without really knowing him. Hadn't he hunted her down night after night and then followed her home?

So she had to decide how much to tell him. Be honest and never see him again? Or lie and hate herself?

She was saved from having to answer Zee's question by a knock on the mudroom door.

"Be right back." She wiped her hands on a nearby towel and went to answer the door. She knew that it could only be Mrs. Mackleworth, and even though she liked her neighbor she wished the woman hadn't chosen tonight for a visit.

She waited a moment, then opened the door with a wide smile.

"Mackey, how nice to see you." Pandora held the door open. "Would you like to come in?" Please say no, she begged silently. But her neighbor bustled inside.

"How are you, dear? I just wanted to swing by and see how you're doing. I'm dying to hear if you've seen that handsome young man again."

"Uh, actually Mackey, Zee's in the kitchen now. I was just putting together some supper for us. Would you care to join us? I'm sure there'll be plenty for three."

Mrs. Mackleworth stopped in the middle of taking off her cloak and stiffened. Her eyes darted toward the kitchen door.

"He's here? Now?" she whispered loudly. "Dear me. I think I left my tea kettle on. I'd better go check." She shrugged her cloak back on and was out the door before Pandora could blink.

Bemused, she walked back into the kitchen.

"Who was that?" Zee asked. "Her voice sounded a little familiar."

"My neighbor, Mrs. Mackleworth. She came to visit but high-tailed it out the door when I told her you were here. I even invited her to dinner, and given her size I know she loves to eat. I'm surprised she left actually. She seems very curious about you."

"Curious about me? Does she know me?" Zee carried his wine

glass over to the table where Pandora worked the crust into a deep pie dish and sat.

He enjoyed watching people who knew what they were doing work. There was something soothing about the way Pandora gently patted and worked the raw dough until it conformed perfectly to the dish.

He looked up to find Pandora blushing.

"I don't think she knows you," she said carefully. "But she came to visit the night—the night you . . . ah, first kissed me and I told her about you."

Unable to look him in the eyes, she kept her head down, focused on the pie dough, and missed the look of enormous satisfaction that filled Zee's face.

"You told your neighbor about me. Interesting. Did you also tell her that I kissed you?"

Pandora turned away from the table and grabbed the pan of hot filling. She poured it into the waiting crust, flipped on the top crust and fluted the edges, then popped it into the Aga's oven.

"Pandora?"

"Mmmm? What?" Why did the man have to ask so many uncomfortable questions? Why couldn't he be like the other loser men she had dated and talk about foolish, inconsequential matters?

Because Zee wasn't a loser, she admitted. And that was why, despite her determination to label him a Player, what Zee thought about her mattered to Pandora. It mattered a lot.

Zee handed Pandora her wine glass. "We need to talk."

"Crap." Why did those words sound so ominous? Pandora took a large swallow of the wine. "All right, if you insist. Let me set the timer for the pie and we'll sit by the fire."

Zee stirred the embers and placed several logs on the always-burning fire. The flames shot up and sparks flew and popped before it settled into a steady blaze. Squirt hissed at the popping embers, then sat on the warm hearth rug to wash.

"What do you want to talk about?" She couldn't keep the sulkiness from her voice and scowled when Zee grinned at her. The man didn't miss a thing, she thought with a huff.

"Why don't you tell me about your family to start. Why do you live in this huge place all by yourself?"

"That's easy. My family is dead. There's only me left."

Zee had hoped for a bit more than that but he let it slide for the moment. He considered her over his wine glass and decided to go for the big question, the one he really wanted answered.

"Why do you roam the city every night?" He watched her hand tremble lightly and the wine slosh in her glass. Hitting a nerve there, he thought. Would she answer him?

"What makes you think I wander the city at night?" Pandora tried to sound haughty, like his question was stupid, but her voice cracked slightly and she knew she hadn't pulled it off.

She couldn't lie. It wasn't in her DNA to lie. And suddenly she didn't want to lie. She was attracted to Zee in a way that befuddled her, but the truth was, she had never before met a man who interested her and made her want the way she wanted Zee.

If he was a Player, well then she'd been played. It was time to lay her cards on the table. She took a deep breath, let it out on a long sigh, set down her wine glass and turned in the chair to face him.

"Okay. Truth time. If you don't believe me or don't like what you hear you know where the door is. You won't be the first to run off after I have my say."

"I'm not leaving without some of that delicious smelling pie." The comment elicited a small smile as he'd intended it to.

"Okay. You'll get pie first, I promise." She twisted her fingers together then dropped her hands in her lap. It was never easy, telling someone who she was. None before had ever believed her. Would Zee be different?

"So, as I told you, my name is Pandora Jones. I come from a long line of Pandoras, going all the way back to the original one. You know, the woman of legend who opened the box—only it was actually a jar—and let all the bad things loose on mankind. We, the original's direct descendants, feel terrible about that and we have tried to atone for it ever since.

"Like every Pandora before me, I go out each night when people's worries are at their strongest and gather the worst ones I can find. I bring them home and secure them in the special boxes that I make."

She shrugged. "That's pretty much my life. Until I found Luke. Now I have another way to help."

Pandora picked up her wine glass and took a big swallow. She braced herself and knew she had to ask. Had to know what Zee was made of. She risked a look at him. He was watching her intently, his smoky gray eyes revealing nothing.

"Will you run screaming from the crazy woman's house now or would you still like some of that pie?"

"Shoot, I told you I'm not leaving without pie. Did you make cranberry sauce to go with it?"

The knot around Pandora's heart loosened a bit and she let out a half-laugh.

"Yes, there's cranberry sauce. My mother taught me that one cannot eat chicken or turkey without offering cranberry sauce."

"Your mother was a wise woman. Were you close?"

"She *was* a wise woman," Pandora said, a wistful expression on her face. "Much wiser than me, I'm sorry to say. I loved her very much and I still miss her every day. I didn't have friends like normal little girls do, so she was not only my mother, she was my best friend. She would've liked you, I think."

"Yeah?" The observation pleased Zee. He reached over and

grasped Pandora's hand, twining his fingers with hers. She looked down at their clasped hands and smiled shyly at him. That was all it took.

Zee tugged her out of her chair and onto his lap, wrapped his arms around her and pulled her close.

Her story sounded crazy, but he had watched her do her oddly seductive dance with her hands outside of strangers's homes late at night. He had seen that she passed by people in her cape without being noticed.

And he knew the tale of Pandora. Hell, the original jar of worries had come from Zee's father.

He lifted her chin with one hand and gently pressed his lips to hers. She sighed and her bare arms wrapped around his neck. The feel of her flesh against the back of Zee's neck sent shivers down his spine.

He deepened the kiss and felt Pandora press tighter against his chest. He ran his hands down her sides, feeling the slim strength of her torso. His right thumb caught the outer edge of a breast and she moaned into his mouth.

Pandora had never felt such pleasure. To be held by the strong and handsome Zee was unlike anything she had ever experienced. She wanted to get closer to him and pressed herself tight against his hard chest.

She loosened her arms from his neck and plunged her fingers into his thick, silky hair. When he groaned in response she realized that Zee wasn't the only one with power. She could make him feel things too.

He parted her lips with his tongue and she relaxed her mouth. When he thrust his tongue inside she met him with enthusiasm and returned the favor.

The kitchen timer buzzed. Zee groaned and swore and Pandora let out a breathless laugh. She sprang from Zee's lap and went to check on the pie.

Her legs felt wobbly and her mind was reeling. This wasn't her first kiss. She had kissed a couple of her past dates, mostly out of curiosity. They had been dry, almost brotherly kisses that had left her feeling relieved when they were done.

Zee's kisses made her feel as if she were about to burst into flames.

While they ate her dinner they kept their talk general, about the city of La Crosse and its history, about Luke and the gangs of thieves that roamed the city.

After their fill of excellent chicken pot pie they sat beside the fire again with bowls of locally made coffee ice cream. When they finished their dessert Zee pulled Pandora onto his lap again and simply held her, stroking her hair, enjoying the contentment of a full stomach, a warm, crackling fire, and the beautiful woman on his lap.

"You have to leave," Pandora eventually murmured. "I have to go to work."

"Take the night off. Stay with me. Let me spend the night."

Oh, how she wanted to do just that! To have a night where she didn't have to face mankind's troubles. A night to follow Zee's kisses wherever they led. She sighed and placed her palm on his beautiful cheek.

"I wish I could say yes, Zee, I really do. But I have to work. I've never missed a night, not since my mother started training me when I was seven. It's not just what I do, it's who I am. You have to go."

Zee turned his face and planted a kiss on her palm. "All right, I'll leave on one condition."

"What's that?"

"Tomorrow you have to take a ride with me on my bike."

Pandora frowned. "What? Like on your handlebars or something? I don't think so."

Zee laughed and planted a light kiss on her scowling lips. "No, silly. On my Harley. I'll pick you up around eleven. We'll take a drive along the river and find someplace to have lunch."

"Ooooh, a *motor*bike! I've never been on one. I'd love to take a ride with you." Pandora hesitated. "Are you sure you want to see me again after what I've told you? I'm not—not exactly your average girl."

Zee stood easily with Pandora in his arms and set her on her feet. He kissed the tip of her straight, regal nose.

"Honey, it's because you aren't average that I want to see you again." And that was the key, he realized. Pandora intrigued him. Not only was she beautiful, sexy, and intelligent, but she had layers to her that he wanted to discover.

She gave him a brilliant smile. "Okay, then. Eleven tomorrow. I look forward to it."

Somehow, the knowledge that she would be seeing Zee on the morrow made the night's gathering of worries lighter work than usual. Pandora practically flew from house to house and at the end of the night secured the collected troubles into their box with a smile before heading to bed to dream of a handsome man with smoke gray eyes.

CHAPTER 20

Zee roared into Pandora's yard at eleven on the dot. The motor-cycle was one of the most beautiful machines she had ever seen. Big, sleek and powerful, just like its owner. Shiny black, with chrome that nearly blinded the eye and burgundy/gold lightning bolts slashed across the gas tank, the bike was the picture of male testosterone.

Eyeing the rider with a flutter in her chest, she had to say the same for its owner.

Clad in form-fitting black leather pants and a matching jacket that had the burgundy lightning bolts repeated across the biceps, Zee managed to look stylish and dangerous at the same time.

She could barely catch her breath when all that gorgeous male walked toward her and smiled. He took her hands and kissed her lightly on the lips.

"Ready?" he asked.

Not trusting her voice, Pandora could only nod.

Zee's smile widened. He led her to the bike, then undid a package wrapped in a pair of bungee cords from the rear of the seat and handed Pandora the contents.

"What's this?" she asked, holding the soft package carefully. A gift? She pressed her lips together to keep them from trembling. Had anyone, besides Mrs. Mackleworth, ever given her a gift before?

Other than her cloak, which she had to have in order to help her mother, Pandora had never received a real present—even on her birthdays. Life was too serious to waste time or money on gifts. Her mother had taught her that.

Her hands shook as she pulled off the string wrapped around the large brown paper grocery bag.

Reaching into the bag, Pandora pulled out a jacket made from black leather as supple as melted butter, with a shiny asymmetrical zipper and a notched collar decorated with stainless studs.

"Oh, Zee. It's so beautiful." Eyes shining with pleasure she quickly put it on. The jacket fit like it had been made for her.

It couldn't be a gift, she thought, running her hands down the supple leather. She'd never felt anything so fine.

Zee must mean for her to use the jacket while they rode because black leather was what Harley riders wore. Being a stylish guy, he would want his passenger to be dressed appropriately.

Well, she would enjoy it while it was hers to use.

"Like it?"

Pandora looked up at Zee. "It's incredible. So soft. I'll be careful with it, I promise."

Zee tugged her long braid out from beneath the jacket and handed her a black helmet also decorated with the burgundy/gold lightning bolts.

"What's with the lightening bolts?" she asked. "I like them."

"You might say it's a family thing," Zee answered with a smile. "The helmets are linked, so we can talk to each other without having to shout," he explained as he helped her fit the chin strap. "This time of year there are a lot of bugs in the air. It takes some of the fun out of riding when they get stuck in your teeth."

Pandora laughed and felt more at ease. "How do I look?" she asked, and did a slow twirl, arms extended.

"Smoking," Zee replied. "I don't think I've ever seen a sexier biker chick." That was the solid truth, he mused. With her long legs clad in snug jeans and the form-fitting jacket Pandora could be a model for a hot Harley ad.

"Biker chick! That's me! Which way are we headed?" Her brow furrowed. "I almost forgot, I have to be back before Luke comes."

Zee kissed the tip of her nose and lowered the helmet's clear shield. He was growing quite fond of that nose. "Not to worry. We'll be back in plenty of time for Luke."

Zee took them along the river, through picturesque and quaint old river towns. They toured the Trempeleau Wildlife Reserve and watched migrating flocks of birds, deer, and tom turkeys strutting for the hens.

"People always think that it's the woman who gets gussied up for men, but it's really the male of the species who likes to preen and strut," she said, as a large tom fanned his magnificent tail.

Zee's laugh made her feel witty and clever, more new emotions to add to this day of firsts.

Pandora had never had so much fun. With her arms wrapped around Zee's trim waist, the sensation of straddling all that throbbing Harley power between her legs thrilled her in a way she recognized as. . . well, sexual was the only way she could describe it.

They lunched at a small diner with an outside deck that hung out over the Mississippi, ate burgers with thick-cut fries and coffee milkshakes while they watched tugboats push huge barges up and down the river.

Pleasure boats filled with fishermen and families out enjoying the gifts of the great river plied the sparkling waters. Puffy white clouds sailed across a deep blue sky and bald eagles soared overhead. Across the wide river steep bluffs rose on the Minnesota side.

Pandora had never felt so relaxed.

They talked and laughed, stopped for ice cream (a treat they both favored), and rolled back into Pandora's driveway a half hour before Luke was due to show up.

Pandora's legs wobbled a bit when she slid off the bike. She laughed at herself, unzipped the jacket and held it out to Zee.

"Thank you for the best day of my life," she said. "I've never had so much fun."

Zee frowned at the jacket. "What are you doing?"

"Returning your jacket, of course."

"Why? It's yours. I bought it especially for you. I don't want it back."

Pandora pulled the jacket to her chest. "It's mine? You-you bought it for me?" she echoed.

Still straddling the bike, Zee grasped Pandora's upper arms and pulled her close. He grinned down at her and she felt her toes curl inside her boots. The man's smile was lethal to her composure.

"I can't think of anyone I'd rather have riding with her arms wrapped around me, Pandora," he said softly, then leaned down and kissed her thoroughly.

When he broke the kiss his eyes were a cloudy gray, more fog than smoke. "You have no idea what you do to me, have you?" he said softly.

Her lips on fire, Pandora could only shake her head in response.

Zee heaved a sigh and set her away from him. "Unfortunately Luke is about to arrive so we can't pursue this conversation. I won't be by tonight, I have some thing's to catch up on. Tomorrow?"

Pandora finally found her voice. "Yes. Tomorrow's great. I'll cook dinner. And Zee? Thank you again for everything. And for the jacket. I love it."

And I'm pretty sure I love you, she mused as she watched Zee ride off. She knew it wasn't smart. A smart woman wouldn't fall for a Player.

She didn't care if Zee was a Player, she realized. The last few days had been the very best of her life, and if it meant that she would have her heart broken when Zee was finished with her, well, it would be worth it.

She buried her nose in the jacket and inhaled its scent. At least now she knew what it felt like to be in love.

CHAPTER 21

PANDORA AND LUKE were scraping old, flaked paint off the carriage house doors and windows when Zee rolled into the driveway on his bicycle the next afternoon.

It was a typical spring day in La Crosse. The air was soft and warm with just a hint of leftover winter coolness blowing off the river, the sun shone bright in a cloudless sky and the sound of traffic on Winter Street was constant but muted behind the great stone mansion.

Zee greeted them and asked for a scraper, then took a spot next to Luke and helped scrape while he asked the young boy about his day.

Luke responded to Zee in a different way than he did to her, Pandora noticed. While he treated her with respect and seemed to like her, when Zee was around Luke positively lit up.

She watched them work side by side on the wide doors, marveling at the way Luke chattered practically nonstop to Zee. Luke answered her questions readily enough when she asked about something, but he didn't volunteer information.

With Zee it was as if some pent-up dam had burst, and Luke couldn't get his thoughts out fast enough.

The kid obviously missed having a man in his life, she mused. She moved off slightly to work on a nearby window to give them space. Zee turned his head and flashed her a smile, almost as if he had read her mind.

What was in it for Zee? she wondered. He didn't have to come this early. He could wait and show up after Luke went home. But other than the previous day after their ride, Zee had been here every afternoon to visit with Luke.

It was as if he recognized the boy's need and had taken it upon himself to fill it.

Pandora frowned at her reflection in the window. What would happen to Luke when Zee moved on, as he was bound to do? Players didn't settle down, didn't make commitments. She understood that, and even though she knew she faced heartache with Zee she felt she was making an informed choice.

Luke didn't understand that Zee was a temporary friend, that he would be leaving any day. If Zee became too important to Luke his leaving would be as devastating for Luke as being deserted by his father had been.

She would have to talk with Zee about it tonight, she decided. He needed to start weaning himself from Luke. Maybe only show up every few days.

The thought depressed her. She looked forward to seeing Zee every bit as much as Luke did.

They finished the afternoon's scraping and put the tools away. Zee lifted Luke's bike into the Thunderbird's trunk and they all piled in for the trip down to Luke's house.

As they were driving away after dropping Luke off, Pandora happened to glance in the rearview mirror. What she saw made her slam on the brakes and leap out of the car.

"What's wrong?" Zee asked the empty car. He turned and looked out the rearview window. "Oh, blast."

Pandora pushed past the three boys surrounding Luke and

placed an arm over Luke's shoulder. He felt stiff under her hand, his face pinched and white. She felt the faint tremors wracking his body and her protective instincts kicked into overdrive.

"Got a woman to defend you, huh Luke?" sneered the oldest boy. "That why you quit on us?"

"You three get out of here. Luke works for me now. You have no business with him anymore." Pandora was pleased to note that her voice sounded strong, not shaky like she felt inside.

The oldest boy, a tall, lanky racial mix with dred locks and multiple piercings on his pimply face, turned cold eyes on her.

"Who are you? This ain't none of your business lady, so butt out. Luke works for me."

"My name is Pandora. Who are you?" Pandora didn't like the cold glint in the kid's eyes. Somehow she had to find a way to scare him off Luke.

The kid drew himself up. His sneer grew. "My crew calls me Blade. Can you guess why?" he asked, eyes glittering with malice.

"Luke's got a job to do and he ain't doing it," Blade continued. "He owes us. He owes me. I'm gonna take this bike as a down-payment."

"You touch that bike and I'll break all your fingers." The threat came from behind Blade.

Pandora caught the surprise on Blade's face when he whirled around and saw Zee. A long, thin-bladed knife appeared in his hand. He slashed out at Zee with it.

Zee easily avoided the blade, grabbed Blade's wrist and twisted. Blade dropped the knife and yowled with pain.

"You boys scram before I call the cops. If I see or hear that you've been hassling my friend Luke I'll hunt you down and deal with you one by one. I can promise you that it won't be pretty. You got that?"

Blade's two followers edged away, then took off running.

"Well?" Zee asked. "Looks like your crew is smarter than you are. Pandora, call the cops."

Zee knew she didn't carry a cell phone, but Blade didn't know that. She made a show of searching her pockets for a phone.

Blade glared at Zee. "This isn't over. I'll find out who you are and I'll be waiting for you when you least expect me." He walked off holding his injured wrist close to his body.

Zee crouched down in front of Luke. "You okay, son?" he asked. Luke flung himself at Zee. He wrapped his arms around Zee's neck and buried his face in Zee's shoulder. Luke's thin shoulders shook.

Zee hugged him tight and waited patiently for Luke to compose himself.

If Pandora didn't know she loved Zee before, she couldn't deny it now. Her heart swelled as she watched Zee comfort the young boy.

When Luke stepped away, wiping his eyes and running nose on his forearm, Zee clasped him on the shoulder with one large, strong hand.

"He'll be back, Luke. That type never knows when to quit and move on. You're going to have to expect him to show up any place and at any time. If you see him don't hesitate, call the police. Blade is dangerous. Promise me you'll call for help."

Luke nodded. "Maybe-maybe I need to get a knife too. So I can defend myself."

Zee shook his head. "No, all that will do is give Blade two knives. Tomorrow I'll start teaching you some defensive moves that will give you time to get away."

Luke's eyes were shining with happiness by the time he went into the house.

"Thank you," Pandora said as they walked back to the Thunderbird. "I wasn't sure how to handle Blade and his crew."

Zee looked at her. A corner of his mouth lifted in a half-smile.

"I can't help but notice that that didn't stop you from plowing into them like a mama bear protecting her cub."

Pandora felt her face warm. "I—I—yeah, you're right. That's exactly how I felt." She sighed. "It isn't going to be easy keeping Luke safe from that gang, is it? It's not enough that I'm giving him work."

Zee opened the driver's door for Pandora, then let himself into the passenger side.

"No, it's not enough. The situation will escalate until someone gets hurt or ends up in jail. Unfortunately we can't shadow Luke while he's in school or watch over him while he's home. I'll talk to Officer Stanhope and tell him what's going on. Maybe he can patrol Luke's neighborhood more often."

They were quiet for the rest of the drive back to Winter Street. Pandora parked the T-Bird in its spot inside the carriage house and waited for Zee to close and lock the carriage house doors.

"Do you still want dinner?" she asked. Please say yes, she begged silently. I need your company tonight.

Zee flashed a wide smile. "Are you kidding? Playing the macho hero makes me hungry. Of course I want dinner. What are we having?"

He draped an arm casually over Pandora's shoulder as they made their way to the house. Happy that he had chosen to stay with her, she reached up and laced her fingers with his and leaned into him.

It felt good having someone to talk with, someone who knew what was going on in her life. Someone she could be honest and open with.

It felt better to have that someone be Zee.

Player, she reminded herself. But instead of a warning shout, the voice was a soft whisper.

CHAPTER 22

DINNER CONSISTED of pasta with fresh vegetables in a cream sauce and lemon meringue pie. Zee groaned when he licked his fork and pushed away from the table.

"You sure can cook, sweetheart. Did your mother teach you?"

Pandora poured the last of the wine into their glasses and handed Zee his. They headed for the chairs in front of the fire and settled in.

Like an old married couple, Pandora mused. "Self-taught, I'm afraid. Mom didn't have time to cook anything more than simple meals. After she died I needed something to occupy my mind so I borrowed cooking books from the library and experimented until I found the foods that I like to make and eat."

Zee patted his full belly. "A man could get used to eating like that."

He stared into the fire and wondered at how unexpectedly right it felt to be sitting there next to Pandora in a house packed to the rafters with boxes of worries.

After he'd dropped her off the previous day he'd gone home to think. He had lied when he told her he had things to do—after spending the day with her he simply needed an evening alone to sort out his feelings.

He had been surprised by how lonely he had felt without her arms around him and her body pressed to his back as he drove the Harley home. And even more surprised by the way he prowled his rental, unable to settle anywhere, wishing he was sitting with Pandora by her fire.

Somehow the woman had gotten under his armor. He never, never ever, let a woman become important. And yet somehow, while he wasn't paying attention, this one had moved to the top of the list of important people in his life.

Zee set his wine glass down and stood. He took Pandora's glass from her hand and pulled her to her feet and into his arms, gratified that she came without resistance.

Pandora lifted her face, a question in her beautiful deep blue eyes. Eyes a man could get lost in, he mused as he lowered his face to hers and brushed her lips lightly with his own. He felt her soften beneath him and lean into him.

That was all it took. Zee pulled her strong, lean body hard against his own and plunged into the kiss. She moaned softly and he was lost.

He broke the kiss to lift her in his arms and carried her to the couch. Setting her down gently, he lay beside her and ran his hand up her long thigh, over her hip, and under her shirt. Over smooth, bare flesh.

He felt her slim waist, her rib cage, and cupped one small firm breast in his hand. He rubbed his thumb over her nipple and felt it harden in response.

Pandora trembled at his touch. Everything in her tightened and yearned at the same time. Never had a man made her burn with desire the way Zee did.

She kissed him eagerly and ran her free hand over his solid chest and back.

"Too many clothes," she said against his throat. She felt his chuckle rumble in his throat and chest.

"My thoughts exactly." They tore at each other's clothing until Pandora lay naked in his arms. Zee turned and supported himself over her, drinking her in.

"Oh my god, you're magnificent," she whispered as she ran her hands over his firmly muscled back and buttocks. She felt Zee tremble at her touch and reveled in the knowledge that she could affect him as much as he did her.

"Make love to me, Zee. Please."

"That's the plan," he answered, his eyes burning with heat and want. He lowered himself enough to kiss Pandora's temple and run kisses down her cheek and around her neck. She arched against him and pulled him closer.

Zee took his time, bringing her to the brink and over several times before he allowed himself to ease into her. He felt her tense and he withdrew, eased further in. When he reached the point where he couldn't hold back any longer he grasped her hips tightly and plunged deep.

Pandora cried out. The unexpected pain was a surprise after all the pleasure Zee had given her.

He stilled inside her, lifted himself, and looked into her face. "Did I hurt you?"

Pandora shook her head, her blue eyes nearly blind with passion. "No. Please don't stop. It's getting more comfortable now." She lifted her head and nipped him on the chin. "Don't leave me hanging. I want to see how this ends."

Zee narrowed his eyes but decided to let it go for the moment. He kept his strokes slow and deliberate until he sensed that Pandora teetered on the brink again, then let himself go. They went over the edge together, panting, held tight in each other's arms.

Zee woke a while later on his back with Pandora draped over

his body. He ran a hand down her graceful back and bottom. She sighed and kissed his throat.

"That was the most amazing thing I've ever experienced," she murmured.

"I didn't mean to hurt you." He felt her shrug a shoulder.

"I've read that some virgins experience a moment of pain. I guess I'm one of them."

Zee tensed. His hand gripped her bottom. "Virgin? You're a virgin?"

"Was." Pandora laughed softly and wrapped one arm around his neck. "Not one anymore, thank you very much."

"Well, blast. I have a rule against bedding virgins." He felt Pandora smile against his throat.

"Then we were each other's first? I like that."

"Huh." The tension slowly left Zee's body. "You know, I think I like that too." He definitely liked that Pandora hadn't been with anyone but him. He was feeling very possessive, a new emotion for him.

He didn't have long to dwell on it as Pandora was busy exploring him with her mouth and tongue. The girl learned fast, he had to give her that, he mused as he found himself ready for another bout of love-making.

CHAPTER 23

ANOTHER WEEK PASSED. Zee and Luke showed up each afternoon and the three of them worked on whatever project Pandora had decided on for the day. They took Luke home together, returned to Winter Street and had dinner, and made love in front of the fire each night.

Pandora was blind with love. She refused to think about the day Zee would leave and even began to hope that he might decide to stay. That hope was dashed exactly one week from the day Zee had chased off Blade and they had first made love, when Zee showed up at Pandora's house with an odd wariness in his eyes.

Pandora said nothing until after they'd seen Luke home and were settled in her kitchen. Instead of prepping dinner, she took a seat across from Zee at the table.

"What's wrong, Zee?" Her stomach clenched into a tight little ball of ice and her blood seemed to freeze in her veins. She knew what was coming. Zee was bored with her and had decided it was time to leave La Crosse.

She wouldn't cry until after he left, she promised herself. She would not let him see how much his leaving hurt.

"I talked to my father this morning," Zee said, breaking into her thoughts.

Ah, Zee's father had demanded his son's return. At least it wasn't completely his choice to leave her. She reached across the table and gently covered one of his fists with her hand.

"I'm listening," she said. "He needs you to come home?" Please don't leave, she begged silently. I need you. I love you.

Zee ran his free hand through his thick hair. "I came here from southern California because Father sent me. He had an errand for me, only he didn't get around to telling me what the errand was until this morning."

Pandora blinked in confusion. "Errand? Kind of like a mission? Are you some sort of spy or something?"

Spies went on missions. Who else? she wondered. Missionaries. Fanatics. People with a dream or purpose in life. Sort of like her, she realized. Her entire life was a mission.

"No, I'm not a spy." Zee hesitated. "About this errand he asked me to do for him . . ." For the first time in his life, Zee had an attack of nerves.

"Look, it's like this. My father is Zeus. My name is also Zeus, but everyone calls me Zee to avoid confusion."

"Zeus? Your name is Zeus?" Her head began to pound and a black fog crept into the edges of Pandora's vision.

"Yes, my name is Zeus. Pandora, my father sent me to find you and get you to stop collecting worries. He says that it's gone on long enough. It was never meant to go this far."

"What do you mean, Zee?" She felt blindsided. Of all the things Zee could've told her, this one wasn't anywhere on her radar. Her words felt strangled in her throat, her chest tight, like it was being squeezed by a giant's fist.

Zee looked at her, his eyes the steely gray of a cold, rainy day. "My father wanted to punish Prometheus for stealing fire and giving it to humankind. He gave Pandora with the jar of ills to

Uncle Prom's brother, Epimetheus. Pandora opened the jar out of curiosity, not malice. She never meant any harm."

Pandora snatched her hand away as if it had been scorched. She took a deep, shuddering breath and pushed her chair back.

"I know she didn't mean any harm," she snapped. "She didn't know what was in the jar. Are you telling me your father set her up?"

Zee waved a hand impatiently. "Not my father, obviously. The original Zeus."

"You're telling me that your family is responsible for all the troubles in the world, not mine?" She stood abruptly, swayed. The chair fell back to the floor with a bang that sent Squirt skittering out of the room, tail high.

Pandora placed her palms flat on the table to steady herself and leaned toward Zee.

"The women of my family have been trying to make up for that innocent act FOREVER. Not one of us has been able to live a normal life because of what your family did."

Pandora straightened. She lifted a trembling arm and pointed toward the door. "I want you out of here. I never want to see you again."

Zee's temper flared. He stood and placed his hands on the table and leaned forward until they stood nose to nose. "Listen to me. I'm trying to do the right thing here," he began.

"Out. You've known who I am all this time. You don't care about me. You're simply following your father's orders. I get that —it's a family thing. But I don't have to like it. You tricked me, Zee. You made me fall in love with you."

Zee's mouth opened and closed but no words came out. He was angry—bloody angry—but he wasn't sure who he was angry with. Himself? His father? Prometheus? The first Zeus? Pandora?

Pandora turned away from the table and walked stiffly to the mudroom door. She held it open. Zee followed her, still fuming.

"Get out. Don't come back," she said in a low voice without looking at him. All the anger had drained from her. She just wanted Zee to leave before he heard her heart breaking.

For a brief moment she thought he was going to refuse to leave and she almost wanted him to stay. Then he moved to the door.

"I'm sorry, Pandora," he said quietly. "I honestly had no idea until this morning."

Pandora closed the door behind him and collapsed against it. The pain in her chest made it hard to breathe. Squirt leaped onto her calf and hung there, mewling piteously. She plucked him up and buried her face in his fur.

"He was The One, Squirt. Now what do we do?"

CHAPTER 24

Zee returned to riding his bicycle around the city of La Crosse late at night. He felt edgy and ill at ease and movement seemed the only thing to help. He pushed himself to the point of exhaustion each night so he could sleep, but his sleep was filled with dreams about Pandora.

His anger still simmered and he *still* didn't know where to direct it.

In general his life bloody sucked at the moment.

Pauli called and he told his brother about the situation. When Pauli pointed out that it was obvious Zee had fallen in love with Pandora Zee hung up on his brother.

His mother called and tried to convince him to go see Pandora again. He cut her off and said goodbye as quickly as he could.

His father called and told him not to return home until he completed his errand.

The problem was that while he really did want to see Pandora again, he wasn't sure she would see him, and he didn't think he could deal with the rejection. As long as he didn't see her he could hope to find a way to work things out.

Meanwhile, the need to see her again ate at him until it consumed every other thought.

He missed the way he felt at home sitting before her fire in one of the worn leather chairs with a glass of wine while she carved on her latest box and they talked. He felt more at home there than he'd ever felt anyplace, including the family houses.

He missed her subtle sense of humor, her do-gooder attitude, her fierce protectiveness of Luke. Blast it, he even missed Luke and the goofy kitten.

Being with Pandora felt right. Holding her in his arms felt right. Making love to her felt right.

So why hadn't he gone back there?

Zee pushed the bike into a higher gear to increase the resistance. He pedaled until his thighs and calves burned while he pondered the question.

He didn't like the answer he came up with.

Pandora tapped the lid onto the paint can with a small hammer and wiped her hands on the rag hanging from her back pocket. She stepped back from the carriage house and cast a critical eye over the freshly painted doors. The deep blue-green doors contrasted well with the pale limestone walls and echoed the soothing greens of the mansion's grounds.

"Good job, Luke. It looks even better than I'd hoped. Nice color choice. You did good." She turned to the boy beside her and smiled.

Luke smiled back but without his usual enthusiasm. They were both hurting without Zee, thought Pandora, not for the first time. When she had told Luke that Zee wouldn't be coming by anymore he had merely pressed his lips together and nodded.

She had seen the hurt and disappointment in Luke's eyes and

her heart ached for him. For both of them. Without Zee she felt like a half-deflated balloon, limping along through her days and her nights.

"Luke . . ." she hesitated. Luke looked at her but said nothing. Pandora knew that he believed it was her fault that Zee no longer came to see them, and he was right. She was the one who had told Zee to leave and never come back.

She had been so hurt that night. Zee's family had caused her ancestors—had caused *her*—an immeasurable amount of suffering. Because of his family the burden of guilt her ancestors carried through the centuries had been great, all-consuming. Almost too much to carry.

How did you explain to a human child the whims and actions of the gods?

Pandora sighed and picked up the paint can and brushes. "I'll give you a lift home," was all she said.

"No thank you, Miss Pandora. I'll ride my bike. Do you want me to come by tomorrow?"

"If it works for you, Luke, yes, I'd like to see you tomorrow. I have a new project in mind." What, she didn't know yet, but she'd come up with something before the next afternoon.

Something fun, she promised silently, that they hadn't done with Zee so his shadow wouldn't be hanging over them.

Later that night, Pandora pulled her cloak around her shoulders, set Squirt inside his pocket, and headed out.

Zee had told Pandora that Zeus wanted her to stop collecting people's worries, but the sad truth was that she wouldn't know what to do with herself if she stopped. Collecting worries was all she knew. It had become her life.

Not her entire life, she amended. She had Luke to think of now, and Squirt. A boy and a kitten. Did that make her pathetic?

She moved through neighborhoods, looking for the strongest,

most debilitating, worries and carefully wound them into small balls and tucked them securely into one of her pockets.

The sense of satisfaction that usually fueled her nights failed to appear. She made her way to Riverside Park, her go-to place when she felt blue, and sat on one of the slatted wooden benches that lined the waterfront.

Her throat burned with sobs that tried to force their way out. Her eyes flooded with unshed tears. She felt thoroughly miserable.

Across the river, an owl hooted in the woods that covered Pettibone Island. Another answered from the woods to her right, north of the paddleboat dock. Water sluiced softly over the banks of the river. The sky overhead shone with countless stars.

None of it lifted Pandora's depression. She plucked Squirt from his pocket and watched him chase insects until he tired and mewed to be picked up.

She missed Zee. His absence had created a hole in her life big enough for the river to flow through. Maybe she'd been a little hasty to banish him. She should have at least discussed the situation with him. Instead, she'd been so shocked by his identity that she had allowed her emotions to rule.

Was he still in La Crosse, or had he left? she wondered. His errand was only semi-accomplished. *I tried to tell the crazy witch to stop with the worries but she tossed me out on my ear.* She could hear him now, complaining to his father.

Zeus. Zee was the next Zeus. No wonder he was so magnificent—he was no mere mortal man. She shivered at the memory of his arms holding her tight to his perfect body.

She should have seen that he was someone special, but she was so busy falling in love with him that she never looked at him clearly. Her vision had been tainted by her need and the spell he seemed to cast over her whenever he was near.

She had entertained a god in her bed—well, on her couch

really—and then she had tossed him out. *Can you spell F-O-O-L, Pandora?*

She scooted down on the bench and leaned her head against the back to look up at the stars. So many possible worlds out there. She used to dream up stories about distant worlds when she was feeling especially lonely and blue. Tonight even that was beyond her.

Making love with Zee had exceeded her wildest expectations. Their joining together had been nothing short of magical. Zee's incredible power, unexpectedly cloaked in tenderness so gentle it had taken her breath away, had doomed her. There could never be another man after Zee.

She reached inside her cloak and rubbed her palm lightly on her abdomen when it clenched at the memories. Zee had kissed her there. He had kissed her everywhere.

She would never forget the look of blind passion in Zee's beautiful gray eyes as he spilled his seed into her. Never forget her own blissful response.

Pandora sat bolt upright, her hand still on her abdomen. There was new life there, she felt its presence pulsing beneath her hand. Her breath whooshed from her lungs. Her blood ran cold, then fever hot.

Impossible. How could she know so quickly? She pressed her abdomen more firmly and knew the truth. A god had planted his seed within her and it had taken hold. She was going to be a mother.

Pandora's mind blanked for several minutes. The knowledge that she was going to be a mother was too large for her to wrap her mind around. There would be another Pandora—she knew the child would be a girl as the Pandora women only birthed girls.

The next in line.

The next in line for what? she asked herself. Did she wish to foist her lonely life upon her child? Did the tradition have to continue?

The thought of breaking a tradition countless centuries old made her feel dizzy. Did she have what it took to send the next Pandora down a different path? A path that included school and friends and boys? All the things that made up a normal girl's life?

She thought back to Zee's errand. What had he said? She had barely listened, she had been so upset over learning that his family was at the root of her lonely life.

His father wanted the practice of collecting worries stopped, that's what Zee said. The Father of all gods wanted the practice to stop.

A smile spread across Pandora's face. She felt buoyed by a lightness she had never before experienced as the heavy chains of a long tradition dropped away from her. She jumped up from the bench and hurried out of the park.

She needed to speak with Zee. She needed to learn exactly what his father wanted her to do and then, if she had the courage, she needed to tell Zee he was going to be a father.

She might wait on that second part, she mused as she hurried uphill and across town toward Losey Boulevard. Fatherhood wasn't the kind of surprise you just sprang on someone you'd only known for a few weeks.

Her nerves stretched tight, she was disappointed to see that Zee's house sat dark and empty when she reached it. Was he inside, asleep? Or had he already left town? Her stomach dropped. *Please don't let him be gone.*

She cloaked herself in shadow so the neighbors wouldn't mistake her for a thief and crept down the side of Zee's house. She peered into a window and saw a sparsely furnished living room. Two chairs. No couch. No television set. The next room held an empty cot and a wooden crate holding a small lamp.

Would Zee live like this? she wondered. Or were these the furnishings of a new tenant?

She had no way to find out unless she knocked on the door. She peered back into the bedroom. The cot was still empty. Whoever lived here was not at home.

Pandora walked swiftly around the back of the house to the garage. She should have thought of this in the first place, she admonished herself.

She peered into the small, grimy window and saw Zee's big Harley parked in the center of the otherwise empty building.

Relief washed through her, leaving her weak-kneed. Zee wouldn't leave without his beloved Harley. He had to be out riding his bicycle. She would come back in the morning, she decided. She'd swing by the bakery and pick up muffins and they would sit and have a civilized conversation about his father's errand.

And maybe talk about babies.

Satisfied with her new plan, Pandora headed swiftly home, but before she reached her house she felt a familiar worry floating on the air.

She frowned, tried to ignore it, then knew that it had to be serious. Luke had been doing so well since coming to work for her. His mother wouldn't be worried at this time of night unless something terrible had happened.

Pandora changed course and headed south to Luke's house. She stood out front and watched Luke's mother pace the floor. Tension made her movements jerky as she paced the small room and wrung her fingers together. Something was very wrong.

Pandora crept around the house and checked the bedrooms. The younger children were all asleep in their beds. Luke's bed was empty. The bike she had gifted him was gone as well, she realized.

She stood for a few seconds and debated the wisdom of what

she was about to do. She had no choice really. Gathering Luke's mother's worry wouldn't help one little bit tonight. The situation called for a solid hands-on approach.

Pandora ran back to the street and knocked on the front door. It was yanked open within seconds. Luke's mother stood there, her tired eyes filled with fear.

"I-I thought you were the police." She took a deep breath. "Can I help you?"

"My name is Pandora. Luke has been working for me after school the last couple weeks. I-I sensed trouble. Is something wrong? Do you know where your son is? His bicycle is gone."

"I have no idea where Luke is. He should be home. He's a good boy, my Luke." Tears shone in the woman's eyes. Her hand trembled as she pushed limp hair from her face.

"That boy showed up," she continued. "The one from the gang. They had words. I'm afraid for my son, Miss Pandora."

CHAPTER 25

PANDORA PLACED a hand gently on the woman's arm and pulled her onto the front stoop, closing the door behind her so their voices wouldn't wake the younger children.

"What's your name?" Pandora asked quietly.

"Samantha. Most people call me Sam." She gripped Pandora's hand tightly. "I'm afraid to call the police. What if Luke went back to that gang—"

"Shh. Sam, you're absolutely right. Luke *is* a good boy. I don't believe he went looking for trouble. Tell me exactly what happened."

"That older boy, he calls himself Blade, came to the house after supper. Luke went out to talk to him. I had the other four to tend to and the next time I looked out the window Luke's bike was gone and so were Luke and Blade."

Pandora patted Sam's shoulder and gave it a gentle squeeze. The woman felt thin beneath her faded cotton robe.

"Sam, I'm going to go look for Luke. Try not to worry. I'll find him. I have some ideas of where they might be." And when I get my hands on Luke I'm going to give him holy hell, she added silently. One of the terms of their work agreement was that Luke would steer clear of the gangs.

Pandora searched each street for several hours, checking the shadows, watching for Luke, Blade or any other gang members. Nothing. She didn't even see or hear Zee on his bicycle.

Exhausted, she decided to stop by her house for a cup of tea before she continued the search. She slipped through the back hedge without even glancing toward Eleanor's windows. Since Zee, she hadn't felt the need to watch the other woman's social life.

She was halfway across the yard when a sense of impending doom hit her. She clutched her cloak tight to her chest, the collected worries squirming against her body in protest at being clasped too tightly, and raced across the dark yard.

She stood at the back door for several minutes, searching for why she felt spooked. Nothing moved. Her mind must be playing tricks on her, she decided.

Almost too tired to stand, Pandora fumbled with the key. It took several tries to open the mudroom door. Once inside she closed it behind her and removed her cloak, dropped the worries into their waiting box, and set Squirt on the floor.

Squirt's back arched and he hissed as he stared into the kitchen. A strong draft blew over Pandora's face, ruffling tendrils of hair hat had loosened from her braid.

She stopped, confused by Squirt's reaction and the unusual current of air, then walked quietly through the kitchen and peered into the main hall.

The front door stood wide open. Two teenaged boys were opening and tossing boxes onto the front portico and into a jumbled pile that filled the front hall. They had already worked their way through hundreds and hundreds of boxes.

She recognized the taller boy as the gang leader Blade. Disappointment knifed through her until she realized the second boy was not Luke.

"There's nothing here," complained Blade's companion. "Every damn box is empty. We're wasting our time. Let's go before somebody catches us."

"Not yet. The bitch has money. Did you see that bike she gave Luke? It's mine now. The traitor owed me."

Pandora winced as Blade knocked over a nearby stack of boxes with a sweep of his hand. They clattered to the floor, their lids popped open, and she watched, helpless to stop them, as hundreds of worries poured into the hallway and floated out the open door.

The sight the escaping worries nearly buckled her knees. Thousands of worries, painstakingly gathered and tucked away over countless nights, unleashed upon the world again.

"I'm telling you this is a waste of time, Blade. Let's get out of here. This place gives me the creeps. What's that lady want with all these boxes? It's weird, man. She's some kind of whacked hoarder. I seen them on t.v. They're filthy dirty and they never throw anything away cuz they're crazy in the head. I'm outta here."

Blade's companion kicked the fallen boxes out of his way and ran out the door. Blade looked through several more boxes, tossing them down onto the piles growing at his feet.

"There has to be something here," he grumbled. He crushed a delicate balsa wood box beneath his sneaker and grinned.

"You have no right."

The voice came from a small body silhouetted against the streetlamp in the open front door. Pandora's eyes widened when she recognized Luke, hands fisted at his side, a furious scowl on his face.

"You have no right," he repeated as he moved into the hallway.

"You had no right to steal my bike and you have no right to destroy Miss Pandora's property."

Blade stopped opening boxes and sneered at Luke. "Says who, sissy boy? You been hiding behind a woman's skirts. You owe me. I collected. The bitch owes me for interfering with my business and I mean to collect on that too so back off. Run home to your mama."

Pandora watched Luke step further into the hallway.

"She owes you nothing, Blade," he said quietly. "And neither do I. I quit the gang. I gave you everything I stole for you. We're even."

He took a step closer to the taller boy. "You have no right to be here," Luke said, taking another step. "Miss Pandora never did anything to you."

Blade leaned back against a stack of boxes and pulled his knife. He began to flick the blade open and closed in a threatening manner. His eyes glittered with malice.

Pandora took a step closer, careful to remain out of sight. She didn't dare leave to call the police. Her only chance to protect Luke would be to take Blade by surprise.

"So, what's the bitch to you, boy-o? Why do you care if I steal from her?" Blade asked, his voice soft.

"Stealing's wrong. And Miss Pandora is my friend."

Without warning, Blade sprung at Luke, knife extended.

Pandora yelled and rushed into the hallway. Blade wrapped his arm around Luke's neck, pulling the boy to him, and pressed his knife tip beside Luke's eye. He grinned at Pandora. His piercings glinted in the faint light of the streetlamp. He looked like a Mardi Gras ghoul.

"Well, well, if it ain't the lady of the house come to rescue Luke again. Take one more step lady and Luke loses an eye. You wouldn't want that, would you?"

Pandora stopped. She was still ten feet away from Blade and

Luke. Too far to leap before Blade made good on his threat. She forced herself to bury the rage she felt. She had to play this smart if Luke was going to escape unharmed.

"What do you want?" she asked in her best quavering "I'm so afraid" voice.

"That's more like it." Blade jerked his head toward the boxes. "I want your money and your jewels, what else? I'll give you two minutes before I start carving on Luke's pretty face. Starting now."

Pandora fluttered her hands in the air, keeping up the image of a helpless female while she tried to think. Jewels? Shoot, any family jewelry was buried beneath boxes in the upper stories. It could take a week to find them.

"We-I don't have any jewelry. See?" She held up her bare hands and fingered her naked ear lobes. "My family had to sell it off years ago to help pay for the upkeep on this monstrous place."

Blade scowled at her. "Fine. Then give me all the cash you have. And the keys to that fine automobile of yours. You have one minute left."

"I keep any cash in the kitchen, in a box. The T-Bird keys are there too. I'll be right back." Pandora turned to go. Why did Blade want the car keys? Didn't the idiot realize that the police would pick him up in the car as soon as he left? He'd never get away with the theft.

Unless Blade planned to kill or seriously injure her before he made his get away. The thought sent a cold chill over her skin.

"Stop right there, bitch. We'll come with you just to make sure you don't try to sneak out the back way." Blade kept his hand wrapped around Luke's thin neck and pushed him toward Pandora.

The rage she was holding so carefully in check climbed to the surface. She whirled to face Blade and looked him in the eye.

"I would *never* desert Luke. He's my friend. I value him more than any jewels or money that might be in the house." She turned away and stalked into the kitchen with the two boys on her heels.

Squirt hissed and darted under the old buffet. At least he would be safe there. She could easily picture Blade stomping on her tiny kitten because the act would give him pleasure.

She needed a plan. Blade was vindictive, and he would want to leave his mark on Luke to teach the younger boy a lesson. She couldn't let that happen.

She thought about the new life growing inside her. She couldn't let any harm come to her baby either.

"Hello? Pandora? The door was open so I let myself in. We haven't had a chance to chat in a few days—"

Pandora heard the back door close. A few seconds later Mrs. Mackleworth appeared in the kitchen doorway, dressed in a kiwi-green pantsuit with the obligatory matching sandals and layers of necklaces shimmering on her ample chest. She narrowed her eyes at the scene before her. "What's going on?"

Blade pressed his knife into Luke's temple. Drops of blood seeped from beneath it and ran down the side of Luke's face.

"What's going on, fatso, is that this is a robbery. You can have a seat with the skinny bitch." He nodded toward the kitchen table while he eyed Mackey's rings and necklaces. "Take off all your jewelry and toss it over to me or the kid here gets cut up."

Blade was enjoying himself, Pandora realized. As long as he held Luke hostage he knew the women would do what he asked. He held the power and he was grooving on it. Maybe it would make him careless. She could only hope.

She couldn't see any way to free Luke at the moment, but she remained alert and ready to spring if the opportunity presented itself.

Mackey sat at the table and carefully pulled the glittering chains over her head, grumbling all the while. She tossed them toward Blade.

"All right." Blade scooped Mack's jewelry into a pile with his foot. "Looks like I made a wise choice coming here after all. Hands on the table where I can see them."

The women complied. Pandora turned her head to look at Mackey, concerned that the older woman might collapse from fear. She was surprised to catch a twinkle in the older woman's eye. Mackey inched her hand toward Pandora's and lightly touched her pinky finger.

"You can't possibly think you'll get away with this," Mackey said aloud, a slight tremor in her voice.

Her neighbor was playing Blade, Pandora realized. Acting as if she was afraid, just as she had done earlier. She decided to join in. Maybe her neighbor had a plan.

"We'll give you anything you want as long as you promise not to hurt us. Or Luke," Pandora added hastily. She felt a slight breeze around her calves.

Someone had just opened the mudroom door. She strained her ears but heard nothing. Had Blade's companion returned?

CHAPTER 26

A MOMENT later Pandora saw a large shadow move past the mudroom door. Was it Zee? Would he come back after she'd told him she never wanted to see him again?

Zee stood in the mudroom just beside the door to the kitchen. He had noticed the open front door of Pandora's mansion as he was biking down Winter Street and knew immediately that something was wrong. Pandora had told him that she never used the front door because the kitchen and mudroom were the only rooms left that weren't stacked to the ceiling with boxes.

That open front door had made his blood run cold. He resisted the urge to storm into the house through the front and raced around the block instead. He left his bike in Eleanor's parking lot, slipped through the hedge, and crept up to the rear of the house. Hiding behind a large cottonwood, he saw through the back windows that the kitchen was empty.

He was about to sprint to the back door when the young thug who called himself Blade followed Pandora into the kitchen. Blade held a knife to Luke's face.

Fury mixed with fear boiled through Zee's body. Blade would

pay for this, he promised. No one threatened the people Zee cared about and got away unpunished.

He turned and skirted behind the carriage house. It smelled of fresh paint, he noted. Luke and Pandora had finished the project without his help.

He heard a woman's voice call out as he moved down the side of the carriage house. A familiar voice. He peered around the corner just as the woman disappeared through the back door. The door closed behind her.

Zee darted across the yard and flattened his body against the back wall of the house. He peered into the windows and watched as the very large woman stripped off jewelry and tossed it toward Blade. She stepped over to sit next to Pandora at the old scarred table.

Pandora looked unharmed, he noted with relief. Even from this distance he could see the fury that she held in check. Blade had no idea what he was dealing with. The thief had stepped into a hornet's nest.

Zee had no doubt that Pandora would crush him if it wasn't for the fact that Blade held Luke hostage.

Zee opened the back door and closed it silently behind him. He glided across the slate floor until he could see Blade and Luke. Blade held the knife close to Luke's eye. A thin river of blood ran down Luke's face.

Zee didn't hesitate. In two quick, silent strides he stood behind Blade.

"Give it up, Blade."

Blade whirled around but he was too slow. Zee clamped the wrist holding the knife. This time he twisted hard enough to hear bone snap. He picked up the dropped knife and tossed it into the huge kitchen sink.

"I should've done that the first time you pulled a knife on me," he told Blade calmly. "Pandora, call the police. Ask for Officer

Stanhope. Tell him we caught the thieving gang leader red-handed."

Blade began to back away. He turned to run but Luke stuck out a foot and tripped him. Blade sprawled on his face. Squirt hissed and darted out from under the buffet. He swiped at Blade's nose, leaving a long bloody scratch. The thief howled and swore.

Mackey waddled over and plopped herself down on Blade's back.

"Get off me, you fat pig."

Mackey calmly scooped her jewelry toward her and began to put it back on. "Is that any way to talk to your elders?" she asked.

Zee squatted down beside Luke and gently placed his hands on the boy's thin shoulders. "Good move, Luke. You all right, son?"

Luke's eyes were wide, the line of fresh blood bright red against his pasty white face, but he nodded. "I'm okay. You saved us."

"Nah, you guys were doing okay. I just hurried things up a little. We need to talk with the police. Are you up for that?"

Luke nodded. "Can you stay with me?"

"Every step of the way. I'm not going anywhere." He looked straight at Pandora. "I'm not going anywhere," he repeated.

Zee reached down and gave Mackey his free hand and helped her to her feet. He grabbed Blade's good arm. "Get up. You're going for a ride." He hauled Blade out of the kitchen and through the front door with Luke on his heels.

"Mackey, are you okay? I'm so sorry you had to walk in on that. You could have been hurt." Pandora remained seated at the table, afraid her legs wouldn't support her.

Blade had terrified her with the threat to cut out Luke's eye. And having Zee there—he said he wasn't going anywhere, and he looked right at her when he said it. Maybe there was hope for them after all.

"I'm fine dear," her neighbor answered. "It takes a lot to upset old Mackey. That's your handsome young man, I take it?" She filled the tea kettle and prepped several mugs, two with hot chocolate and two with tea balls.

When the tea was ready she carried both mugs to the table and sat beside Pandora. They drank their tea in a comfortable silence and waited for Zee to return. The talk with the police seemed to take forever.

Finally Zee glided back into the kitchen, Luke still at his heels. Mackey batted her eyelashes at him as she fixed the hot chocolate. "Care to introduce me to your friends, Pandora?" she asked.

"Oh, of course, how rude of me. Mackey, this is Zee and my friend Luke. This is my neighbor Mrs. Mackleworth."

"She knows darn well who I am, don't you Aunt Seph?" Zee took the mug of hot chocolate and kissed Mackey on the cheek. "Did you think I wouldn't recognize you under that get-up? Your voice always gives you away."

Aunt Seph? Did Zee know Mrs. Mackleworth? "What's Zee talking about, Mackey?" asked Pandora.

"Come on, Auntie." Zee pointed his finger at Mackey. "Gig's up. Father sent you here to keep an eye on me, didn't he?"

Mackey seemed unperturbed at being outed. She sipped her tea and smiled at Zee. "It was your mother actually. I can't say that I minded. I was bored, and acting the part of Mrs. Mackleworth has been great fun. Now I really must be going. I have a great deal of packing to do. I'll see you both later today." She set her tea mug in the sink and disappeared through the mudroom door.

Pandora watched Mackey go, then looked at Zee, who grinned back at her. Her heart fluttered. She wasn't ready for that conversation yet, she decided.

She turned to Luke, relieved to see that his natural color had returned. "What did the police say, Luke?"

"They arrested Blade. Officer Stanhope is pretty nice. He made Blade tell me where he hid my bike. He said that Blade's going to jail, but because I quit the gang and tried to stop him they won't arrest me for stealing from before."

"That's good. I know your mother is pretty worried about you. Why don't I give you a ride home? We can talk more tomorrow when you come to work."

Luke's eyes widened. "You-you still want me to work for you?"

"Absolutely. You tried to protect me tonight, Luke. You proved that you're my friend. Friends have to stick together. Come on, we'll take the T-Bird and pick up your bicycle on the way."

Zee insisted on accompanying her to Luke's. They were both silent on the way back to Winter Street. Pandora parked the car, locked the carriage house doors, and took a deep breath for courage.

"Don't even think about tossing me out again," Zee said before she could speak. He took her hand in his and twined their fingers, then turned her to face him.

"I wasn't going to toss you out." Pandora looked into Zee's warm eyes. "I was wrong to toss you out before. I'm sorry. I have to admit that I've missed you terribly."

She looked away, afraid of what she might see. Laughter? Aloofness? She couldn't bear either from him. They would mean she'd blown it with the only man who had ever mattered. The only man who ever would matter.

"Missed me, huh?" The softness of his tone gave her hope. He pulled her into his arms and looked down into her face.

"I'm sorry about the boxes, Pandora."

The change of subject rattled her. She had avoided thinking about the boxes. A tight band constricted her chest and made it hard to breathe. Her fear for Luke had driven out the other fear. All those worries, released back into the world.

For years she had spent every night collecting those worries. Her life's work, destroyed in minutes by two ignorant teens.

A tear slid down her cheek. She looked up at Zee. His beautiful gray eyes, soft with sympathy and understanding, undid her. He pulled her to his chest and held her tight as she began to cry big, gulping sobs that shuddered through her entire body.

She cried for the released worries, but she also cried for herself—for her lonely and wasted life.

When the sobs died into hiccups Zee swept her up and carried her into the house. She felt too drained to resist. He sat in one of the fireplace chairs and held her on his lap, then gently lifted her chin and forced her to look at him.

"Believe it or not, I understand what you're feeling, Pandora. Your life's work, and some of your mother's as well, I'll wager, was destroyed by that young thug."

Pandora brushed the last of the tears away from her face with the back of her hands. "Every night of my life since I was seven years old was trapped inside those boxes. I'm not sure how I feel."

Zee pulled her against his chest and stroked Pandora's hair and back until he felt some of the tension leave her body.

"I know you don't, sweetheart. Perhaps this is a sign that it's time to let go of the past and think about building a new future. While it's true that Zeus was angry when he set the original Pandora up, he was never angry with Pandora. He loved her. She was beautiful and warm and intelligent and everything he had asked the lesser gods to create. She was just like you."

"He loved her?" She snuggled closer and breathed in Zee's unique scent. How she'd missed him.

Could she let go of the past and start fresh? she wondered. She had considered doing just that while she sat beside the river and contemplated her baby's future. She hadn't realized exactly what that entailed until she had seen the boxes opened and tossed aside like trash.

"All those things that your ancestor let out of the amphora? They were going to be let loose on the human race anyway." Zee ran a finger along Pandora's jaw. "The bottom line is that the first Pandora just happened to be the instrument Zeus chose so he wouldn't be blamed."

Pandora stiffened and tried to pull away. "What do you mean they were going to be released anyway?" she asked. "Why would Zeus do that? Did he hate mankind?"

Zee's arms tightened around her. Now that he had Pandora where he wanted her—where he *needed* her— he wasn't going to let her leave his lap until she heard everything he had to say.

"The human race needs evil and worries and troubles, sweetheart. Without them people would simply lie around in a complacent, stagnant haze. People need challenges in order to grow, to strive to become more than what they are."

Pandora drummed her fingers on Zee's chest. "Say that's true, then why let generations of my family suffer?" she asked. "How do you give back all those wasted lives?"

"I can't. But if you'll let me, I can change *your* life. That's the only one I care about." Zee lifted Pandora's chin and looked into her beautiful eyes.

That small familiar fluttering started again in her chest.

"I love you, Pandora. Marry me. Please. I need you. There could never be another woman for me as long as you roam the Earth."

The slight flutter in her chest grew to a swarm of butterflies.

"Together we'll open and release all the troubles collected in this house and then we'll sell the boxes," Zee continued. He pressed his lips softly to her chin and each tear-stained cheek. "Those boxes represent a small fortune in fine art. I have connections all over the world who would be happy to sell them in their galleries."

Pandora thought about the thousands of finely wrought boxes that filled four floors of her home and all the troubles they held. Yes, the boxes could be considered art.

Perhaps Zee had a point. And perhaps people did need their worries to show they cared about others, and troubles to overcome to make them feel strong and give them a source of pride.

She could use the proceeds from the sale of the boxes to help families like Luke's. The idea excited her.

"You could find markets for the boxes?" she asked.

Zee's eyes narrowed. The boxes were not what he wanted her to focus on at the moment. Hadn't she heard him propose marriage? Obviously he needed to make her understand that she belonged to him.

Zee lifted her chin again and placed a gentle kiss on her lips. Then deepened it until he felt her respond.

Pandora felt the kiss slide through her body down to her toes. She wrapped her arm around Zee's neck and pulled his head closer. Felt him respond to her. Yes, she thought with satisfaction, this is where he belongs.

Zee broke the kiss. "You haven't answered me," he said, his voice gruff with emotion. "I need an answer, Pandora."

"The answer is yes, Zee. I will marry you."

The relief that shot through Zee's body staggered him for a moment. He hadn't realized how desperate he had been to know that she belonged to him.

"Once the house is emptied of boxes we can fill it with children and friends. We can create a new line of ancestors who change the world in better ways," he said. "What do you think of that idea?"

An emotion Pandora had never felt before expanded inside

her body until she thought her chest was going to crack wide open. It was more than happiness, it was Joy.

She looked into Zee's incredible face, into his silvered, mysterious eyes, and felt more love than she ever dreamed possible. Here was the answer to her own worries, the answer to the dreams she had always feared to voice. The answer to her silent prayers.

"Yes," she whispered, kissing Zee lightly. "Let's start emptying those boxes. As for the children, we've already made a start on that."

Zee froze. He gripped Pandora's arm. "What did you say?" he croaked. "You're-you're—*we're* going to have a baby?"

Her smile widened and she nodded.

Zee whooped and stood with her in his arms. He whirled around the kitchen laughing like a crazy man. He kissed Pandora loudly, then whooped again.

"I guess that means you don't mind getting an early start on our family," she said, and snuggled against his chest.

CHAPTER 27

THE WEDDING TOOK place at Zee's parents' favorite villa in the Italian Alps. Everyone who was anyone attended. Gods, demigods, and mere mortals mingled and partied as if they'd been friends forever.

Mrs. Mackleworth, who was actually Zee's Aunt Persephone, was there and looking quite lovely without her fat suit and outrageous outfits. Dressed in a simple column of gold silk with tasteful jewelry, Pandora was amused to see that she still wore matching Birkenstocks.

Persephone's footwear helped Pandora to remember that gods were people too, with their own set of quirks and peculiarities. She liked Zee's mother Hera, found the elder Zeus to be somewhat intimidating and even more handsome than Zee, and she immediately loved Zee's siblings, his brothers Apollo and Perseus, and his sister Artemis—who insisted Pandora call her Tia.

"Miss Pandora, do you think we could swim in the pool later?" Luke's sister Amy looked up at her, her large brown eyes hopeful in her small triangular face.

Pandora picked Amy up and balanced the tiny girl on her hip, careful not to put pressure on her already growing belly.

"I don't see why not. I'd like to go for a swim myself once everyone leaves. Why don't we find your mother and see what she says?"

Pandora had been ecstatic when Zee offered to fly Luke's family to the wedding. She and Luke's mother Samantha had become good friends over the last few weeks, and it was nice for her to have a few guests of her own amongst all the strangers.

They found Sam, checked with Hera to be sure swimming was okay, and headed out to the athletic field where the games were being held.

"Games at a wedding?" Pandora asked Zee's brother Pauli when she heard about the scheduled events.

Pauli laughed, his strong teeth flashing white in his tanned face, and laid his arm companionably over Pandora's shoulder.

"You'll get used to it. Think about who you're dealing with here. Our people can't get together without some sort of competition to make it interesting. The wedding is another excuse for Father to show off." He waggled his golden eyebrows at her, his eyes laughing.

"Who knows, maybe it's Zee's year to beat him. You know what that means, don't you?"

Pandora looked at Pauli with alarm. "No. What would it mean if Zee won the games?"

Pauli leaned close and whispered in her ear. "It means Zee becomes Father of the gods, of course."

Pandora pulled away from him. "You're kidding."

"Nope."

"Excuse me, Pauli, I have to find Zee before he does something foolish." She hurried off to find her new husband. Change was good, but she preferred to take it in small bits. Becoming

Zee's wife had been a big step. She wasn't yet ready to be the wife of Zeus, Father of the gods.

Later, standing with Zee as they watched Zeus soundly beat his own brothers, Pandora sighed with contentment.

Zee glanced down at her and smiled. "Happy, love?"

Pandora slid her arm around Zee's waist and snuggled close. "Yes. Your family is wonderful. And thank you for inviting Sam and her family. It means a lot to me to have my own friends here."

Zee kissed the top of her head. "I know it does. I've been thinking about when we get home."

"Yes?"

"Well, I know you're a very capable woman, but it seems to me that taking care of that over-sized house of yours will be a huge task, especially once the baby is born."

Pandora's eyes narrowed. "You're not suggesting I sell my family home are you?"

"No. No, no, no. I'm thinking we should offer Sam a job as live-in housekeeper. There's plenty of room for her and the kids on the third floor. That way we'd all be under one roof. We wouldn't worry so much about them."

Pandora threw her arms around Zee and kissed him. "I knew there was a reason I love you. That's a fantastic idea!" She beamed at him. She had everything she could possibly want.

Best of all, one of man's oldest myths finally had a happy ending.

I'm glad you found this book out of the millions available. If you'd like to know when I release a new book instead of leaving it to chance you can sign up for my newsletter or follow me on Facebook. You can also see what I'm working on or even send me an email– all through my website, CharleyMarshBooks.

Turn the page for the first chapter of *Cassandra,* another romance from the Romancing a God series.

CASSANDRA

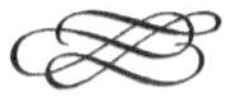

ROMANCING THE GODS

CHARLEY MARSH

CHAPTER 1

CASSANDRA BROWN WHIPPED her ancient Toyota 4Runner into the boatyard's parking lot and headed for the employee's parking area at the far end.

A collection of upscale vehicles already dotted the lot: high dollar SUVs mixed with Mercedes, Cadillacs, Audis, and BMWs, the status symbols of the boat owners who wanted to get in an early sail or time on the water before heading off to their swanky offices in the city.

Cassie pulled into the empty slot between her boss's new Tundra and her friend Amber Day's almost-new Volvo wagon, smirking over the mental picture of her 4Runner as the thorn between two roses.

The music cut out abruptly when she turned off the engine. Although she was already late she sat and listened to the cooling engine's pings and pops.

She rarely listened to tunes at an ear-splitting volume, but she had spent another late evening with her fiancé and his mother and was having trouble waking up. The loud music, while irritating, helped.

Cassie swallowed the last of the still warm coffee in her travel mug and stepped out of the 4Runner. An onshore breeze hit her face immediately, bringing with it the smell of frying donuts from the small waterfront cafe that opened early to accommodate the boaters who hadn't thought to bring something to eat or drink with them.

Her mouth watered at the smell of fried dough and sugar. She had slept through her alarm so hadn't had time for breakfast. Unfortunately, as Jonathan had already scolded her twice last week for tardiness she had no time to grab anything now either.

Cassie pulled her heavy tool bag from the passenger seat and slammed the door. It bounced open and she slammed it again. She didn't bother locking it. There was nothing of value inside and the 4Runner was by far the crappiest vehicle on the lot. No one would ever try to steal her car—one of the few bennies of being perennially poor.

The tool bag was a pain to lug back and forth every day, but it had been one of the first things she'd made for herself when she'd made the switch from sailmaker to canvas worker and it held practically everything she owned of value.

Constructed of tough navy blue denier on the outside and lined with heavy white canvas, the bag boasted numerous pockets and slots for everything she needed to do her job. A heavy duty zipper ran along three sides and allowed her to spread the bag flat for easy access.

It was the most deluxe of tool bags and a fine example of what she was capable of creating, if she did say so herself.

More important, all of the tools inside the bag belonged to her—not the marina—a fact she took pride in. She'd had to save for each and every tool and build her collection slowly, always researching carefully and buying the best quality tool she could find.

Cassie shifted the bag to her other hand. She could have left the bag in the sail loft each night—Jonathan swore no one would mess with it— but she couldn't do it.

To appease Jonathan, who kept harping on it, Cassie had tried leaving the bag in the loft one night. After a sleepless night worrying about her tools she vowed never to leave it again. Pretty much all of Cassie's net worth lived in her tool bag, so she hauled it between work and home.

And she had to admit that if she decided to leave Portland suddenly she would need the bag of tools to start a new life. She hoped that this time she could stay—she always hoped that she could stay—but something always seemed to happen that forced her to pull up whatever shallow roots she'd managed to put down and move on.

She hoped that after the last move she'd learned to keep her mouth shut. No one needed to know that she had visions. Especially not now, not when she was on the verge of forever distancing herself from her lowly beginnings.

The sight of the boats moored in the marina filled her with happiness, especially the ones wearing her canvas. *Her* canvas. Conceived, designed, built and installed by her own hands.

Cassie took her canvas craft seriously and was beginning to build a reputation in the Portland area as a conscientious and skilled fabricator.

It helped that she was female and treated her customers well —unlike the men who owned the area's three other canvas shops. The demand for canvas far outran the supply and the other shops tended to be arrogant, with a "We'll get to you when we get to you, take it or leave it" attitude.

This spring, for the first time since she had started working at Haskell's Marina, people came asking for her specifically. Instead of just asking Jonathan if the sail loft handled the specialty canvas items people liked to buy for their boats, they actually asked for Cassandra Brown.

She couldn't be more thrilled.

Smiling now, Cassie stepped onto the covered walkway that ran the length of the south side of the long, cedar-shingled building and headed for the double doors that opened directly into the sail loft.

The walkway protected customers headed to the marina offices, or Mike's Chandlery—where they could buy everything and anything a boat owner could possibly want—or to Bounty of the Sea, the marina's popular seafood restaurant that looked out over the protected bay that was home to the marina.

The middle of June meant the boating season was in full swing. Portland's boaters wasted no time once winter released its icy grip on Maine's southern coast. The boating season was short and the enthusiasts were dedicated to making the most of it.

Despite being late, Cassie stopped a moment to enjoy the sight. Beyond the large marina building the bay sparkled in the morning sun. Hundreds of white hulls bobbed on their moorings. Sailboats of every size and design, power boats, and fancy sport fishing boats gently rocked and slowly spun in the gentle breeze.

Cassie saw the Boston Whaler the marina used to ferry the boat owners back and forth carefully weaving its way through the moored boats. She squinted at the helmsman. Broad shoulders and sunlight glinting off shiny dark hair told her that Pauli was working the launch this morning.

Good. She needed a ride out to a customer's boat for a fitting as soon as she gathered her things. Of the three launch drivers she liked Pauli best. The other day driver, Amos, was very nice, but there was just something special about Pauli. He had a way about him, an ease with people that she envied since she seldom felt easy around others.

Cassie stopped just inside the sail loft doors to remove her deck shoes and tossed them to the side with everyone else's. The entire sail loft floor was their work table and had to be carefully protected from dirt and scuff marks. Customers were allowed no farther inside than the door, a policy that was fiercely and gleefully policed by the sail makers.

It wasn't often one of the ordinary citizens got the chance to scold and reprimand the wealthy class. They enjoyed it so much that Jonathan had been forced to create a rotation sheet ensuring that they each got a turn.

Cassie loved working in the large, open loft. Bright and airy, with windows on three sides that let in the light and sea breezes, it was a pleasant and inviting space that could easily have held four apartments the size of her own.

Constructed of plywood sheets covered with a dozen coats of polyurethane, the scrupulously clean floor gleamed in the morning sunlight. Five sewing machines were the only obstructions on the bare floor.

The stitchers sat in wooden boxes suspended below floor level, only their torsos and arms visible. The often massive projects were laid out on the floor where they could be moved around and fed through the machines with a minimum of hassle.

It was the nicest sail loft Cassie had ever worked in.

"Morning, Cassie." A heavy-set man in his late twenties called to her from his knees where he was carefully cutting a large sheet of white dacron with a heat knife.

A black symbol stuck onto one corner told her he was working on a new sail for the J series of racing boats that were popular in the area. Most sailmakers added any lettering and numbers at the end; Stan liked to buck the trend and put his on first. He claimed they helped him tell which end was up.

"Hi Stan. How's it going?" Cassie skated across the floor in her thick socks over to the corner that housed her canvas projects.

"Oh, you know. It's going. Jonathan was looking for you earlier. Did he catch you?"

Cassie's heart sunk. There were only two reasons her boss would seek her out: either a customer had a problem, or he wanted to give her another warning about being late.

"Thanks. No I didn't see him. I have to do a fitting once I grab my stuff. Can you tell him I should be back in about two hours?"

"Can and will," Stan replied.

The image of a bewildered Stan standing in an empty apartment flashed into Cassie's mind. Poor Stan. He was a truly nice guy. It sucked that his wife was planning to leave him.

She pushed the image aside. Past experiences had taught her that sharing her visions would not change things. If anything, sharing with Stan would destroy the friendly working relationship that she had going with the man. People didn't appreciate the bearer of bad news.

She forced her brain to concentrate on what she needed for the fitting. The launch operators didn't appreciate it when she had to make extra trips because she forgot something.

Her boss Jonathan liked it even less.

"Every trip costs the marina in wages and gas," he had lectured her the one time she had forgotten to stock her bag with a special fastener the customer had requested. "The next time this happens I'll deduct both from your week's pay."

Cassie had made sure it didn't happen a second time. She needed every penny she took home.

She pulled the cut lengths of blue Sunbrella fabric from their slot and checked the customer name, boat name, and supply list she had clipped to the end.

Originally constructed from tightly woven cotton, modern day canvas was a synthetic that stood up better to the constant wear of salt and sun. Cassie would've preferred to work with cotton canvas, but her customers were educated and wanted the latest hi-tech fabrics.

"You headed out?" Amber Day, sailmaker and friend, called to

Cassie from her sewing box. Lightweight yellow, green, and blue fabric billowed around her upper body. By the end of the day the fabric would be stitched into a complex design, taped and grommeted; a completed spinnaker soon to be seen flashing around the Casco Bay islands.

"Yeah, I have a dodger fitting," Cassie answered. She pulled boxes of snap fittings from a cubbyhole and put them in her bag. Five boxes: two parts to the snap cap, two parts to the snap stud, and one of screw-in studs that attached to the boat. Check. Snap tool. Check.

"Little late getting going, aren't you?"

Cassie looked up at the slight snark she heard in Amber's voice. Since Cassie's engagement last month to Brad Farland III, Esquire she had felt a small wedge in their friendship. She inspected her friend while she wondered how to deal with the growing distance between them.

Amber had pulled her frizzy red hair back in a tight ponytail. Her large green eyes, filled with hurt resentment, looked back at Cassie from a pale, freckled face.

The resentment bothered Cassie. She made every effort to behave as she always had, despite her recent engagement to Portland's most eligible and wealthiest bachelor. She decided the best path was to ignore Amber's snark.

"The wine-tasting went later than I thought it would and I couldn't leave until Brad did. I wish you had come with us. Brad wouldn't have minded."

Amber snorted. "Yeah right. What about Brad's mother? Somehow I'm sure that Portland's most famous society dame would have minded a great deal if you brought an unapproved guest to her shindig."

"You're not—" Cassie stopped. The bitter truth was that Charlotte Farland, queen of Portland society, *would* have minded if Cassie brought Amber with her to the charity tasting.

"Yeah, that's what I thought." Amber bent her head to her sewing machine and fed the flowing fabric through with skilled hands.

Conversation over.

Cassie hurriedly pulled the rest of her supplies together, put her deck shoes back on, and headed for the dock to catch the launch.

Being engaged to Brad wasn't working out quite like she had thought it would. Instead of expanding her circle of friends, it seemed to be having the opposite effect—the number of real friends, a small one to start with, was shrinking.

You can find your copy of Cassandra at your favorite retailer here: https://books2read.com/u/31qQPW